COMFORT OF A MAN

Brooklyn controlled her shock at the direction her thoughts had turned, but Pandora's box had been opened and damn if she could close it.

"So I guess all we have is tonight?" Isaiah asked and lifted a glass to her.

Baby steps.

"I guess so," she answered in a low whisper. Damn, he was good looking. When was the last time she'd been around someone who'd made her feel like a woman—a desirable woman?

She took a deep breath and lifted her glass to him. "Since tonight is all we have, why don't we spend what's left of it up in your suite?"

BOOK YOUR PLACE ON OUR WEBSITE AND MAKE THE ARABESQUE ROMANCE CONNECTION!

We've created a customized website just for our very special Arabesque readers, where you can get the inside scoop on everything that's going on with Arabesque romance novels.

When you come online, you'll have the exciting opportunity to:

- View covers of upcoming books

- Learn about our future publishing schedule (listed by publication month and author)

- Find out when your favorite authors will be visiting a city near you

- Search for and order backlist books

- Check out author bios and background information

- Send e-mail to your favorite authors

- Join us in weekly chats with authors, readers and other guests

- Get writing guidelines

- AND MUCH MORE!

Visit our website at
http://www.arabesquebooks.com

COMFORT OF A MAN

Adrianne Byrd

ARABESQUE

★BET
BOOKS™

BET Publications, LLC
http://www.bet.com
http://www.arabesquebooks.com

ARABESQUE BOOKS are published by

BET Publications, LLC
c/o BET BOOKS
One BET Plaza
1900 W Place NE
Washington, DC 20018-1211

All Kensington Titles, Imprints, and Distributed Lines are available at special quantity discounts for bulk purchases for sales promotions, premiums, fund-raising, and educational or institutional use. Special book excerpts or customized printings can also be created to fit specific needs. For details, write or phone the office of the Kensington special sales manager: Kensington Publishing Corp., 850 Third Avenue, New York, NY 10022, attn: Special Sales Department, Phone: 1-800-221-2647.

First Printing: July 2003
10 9 8 7 6 5 4 3 2 1

Printed in the United States of America

To Alice Finley.
Thanks for always being the wind beneath my wings.

And to Channon Kennedy—
for being a beautiful set of wings.

Baby Steps

One

Brooklyn Douglas sat mute in a crowded New York restaurant while a group of her closest friends discussed her life as though she weren't there. This wasn't the first time such a discussion had occurred—far from it; however, Brooklyn noticed they happened with more regularity than she liked.

"Okay, okay." She leaped into the conversation. "Can we please change the subject?"

Toni turned her suspicious gaze toward Brooklyn. "When was the last time you even got laid?"

Brooklyn's eyes bulged. "Excuse you?"

Toni rolled her eyes, undaunted by her friend's reaction. "Just what I thought."

Brooklyn's other three girlfriends, Ashley, Maria, and Noel, snickered while dodging Brooklyn's lethal gaze.

"What on earth does my getting laid have to do with anything?"

Maria's thick accent sliced into the conversation. "If you don't know, then you're worse off than we thought."

Another round of snickering ensued.

A smile bloomed on Brooklyn's face. "Come on, girls. You know I don't have time for a relationship. With my new career, dealing with Evan's crap, and Jaleel's growing pains—"

"Who said anything about a relationship?" Noel brushed back a wisp of her blond hair as her green eyes twinkled. "Haven't you heard of baby steps?"

"A one-night stand?" Brooklyn concluded in shock. "Me? A one-night stand? You've lost your mind."

Ashley leaned over and draped an arm around Brooklyn's shoulders. "Where is your sense of adventure?"

"An adventure is a trip to Africa, not playing Russian roulette with sexually transmitted diseases."

"No one said anything about unprotected sex," Toni reasoned with a dismissive wave. "We're just saying that you need to do something to relax."

"I thought that was the purpose of our trip up here to New York. We came to take in a few Broadway plays and enjoy the city."

"Look," Maria said, smiling. "There's relaxing and then there's *relaxing*. And the kind that you need requires an extra appendage." She wiggled her brows. "Are you catching my drift?"

"Unfortunately."

Maria shook her head. "I don't know why we're bothering. You'll never do it. You're such a prude."

"A prude?" Brooklyn's hands flew to her hips. "That's not true."

Maria raised her hands in surrender. "I don't mean to upset you, but you have to admit you've changed a lot since college."

"Well, who hasn't?" Brooklyn's gaze shifted to each of them. "Noel drank her way through college. Toni was on a mission to sleep with each member on the football team. Ashley—"

"What about me?"

"You"—Brooklyn swiveled in her direction—"you were a walking, talking chimney stack. What was your peak, three packs of cigarettes a day?"

Ashley blanched contritely and slumped back in her chair.

"And you." Brooklyn's attention jerked back to Maria. "I don't think you went on a single date the entire time we were there—including graduate school."

Maria simply shrugged. "What can I say? I was a late bloomer."

"You never bloomed. You didn't get any action until you ran out and bought those silicone twins of yours in Los Angeles."

The other women at the table squealed.

Maria cupped her breasts. "And they were worth every penny."

The laughter escalated.

Brooklyn rocked back in her chair with her hand covering her mouth. It felt good to be out with her friends. In her opinion they didn't get together enough. Life had a strange and powerful way of bringing different people together and then scattering them across the map.

Maria was a big shot at Paramount Pictures out in Los Angeles. Ashley worked at the American embassy in England. Noel resided in New York, working for a record label and being "the only white girl in rap" as her friends liked to tease her.

Brooklyn and Toni lived in Atlanta, a few miles apart; however, they rarely saw each other. But the women were never too far away in their hearts. As close as they were, one member was missing from the group: Macy Patterson.

Macy and Brooklyn were roommates in college. Both were business majors and came from startlingly similar backgrounds. They shared everything: clothes, money—you name it. Then, Macy took sharing too far the day Brooklyn came home early and found her husband in bed with Macy.

"What time is it?" Brooklyn asked, suddenly feeling as though they'd been in the restaurant too long.

Toni looked at her watch and then tossed the napkin from her lap onto the table. "It's seven-thirty. We better get going if we're going to make the eight o'clock show."

The girls stood and donned their coats in preparation for the December wind outside. Each left money for their bill on the table. Nearing the front door, three of them made a sudden turn in the opposite direction.

"We're just going to make a quick trip to the rest room," Noel announced to Brooklyn and Toni. "We'll be right back."

Brooklyn nodded. "Let's just stand over here and wait for them," she said, indicating a small bench in the waiting area. She sat down and Toni tugged her arm. Brooklyn turned toward her.

Toni gave a slight nod over her shoulder. "Do you see what I see?" She nodded again.

Brooklyn's gaze shifted to over her friend's shoulder and to an incredible specimen: a six-foot-three brother with beautiful toffee-colored skin and a physique that caused an instant heat to generate in the core of Brooklyn's body.

The man smiled at the hostess, displaying a stunning set of white teeth, while his shadowy goatee showcased a pair of perfectly arched full lips. His gaze slid toward Brooklyn, and her breath caught at the sight of his clear gray eyes. He smiled and nodded in her direction.

Unable to think of anything else, she mimicked his action before the hostess regained his attention and led him away.

"Ooh, girl," Toni crooned in her ear. "Did you see the way he checked you out? Are you sure you don't want to go do a panties check before we head over to the theater?"

Brooklyn cut her eyes over at her friend and swatted her on the arm. "Very funny."

"Who's trying to be funny? Hell, I may need to do one myself."

Their three friends sauntered around the corner.

"Are you two ready?" Maria asked. Her gaze bounced from Toni to Brooklyn and like always her keen senses zeroed in. "What did we miss?"

"Nothing," Brooklyn hurried to answer in a vain attempt to cut off any explanation from Toni.

Toni laughed as she stood. "You missed a good one, girl. Brooklyn had a seriously fine brother checking her out a few minutes ago."

The other girls perked up as all eyes darted in Brooklyn's direction and a barrage of questions flew her way.

"Did you get the digits?" Ashley asked.

"Did you give him your number?" Maria countered.

"How fine was he?"

Brooklyn held up her hand, which immediately silenced them. "No, no, and he was just all right. Can we go now?"

"Just all right?" Toni barked with laughter, and then shook her head. "Girl, you're hopeless."

The girl's exuberant faces quickly turned sour as they bobbed their heads in agreement.

"Well, let's get going. We're already running late."

Everyone headed toward the door.

Brooklyn brought up the rear, but as she neared the door, she felt as though she was being watched. She glanced over her shoulder and her gaze collided with those sparkling gray eyes from across the room.

The man's lips curled into a smile as he lifted his wineglass and nodded toward her.

She smiled back a second before Noel clamped on to her wrist.

"Will you come on?" Noel said, and pulled her through the door.

Isaiah Washington forced his attention away from the door and the stunning woman who'd walked out of it. He had laughed at but never experienced love at first sight—until now. He shook his head to clear his thoughts. Okay, maybe love was overstating it a bit, but there had been something there—a spark, an attraction?

"Isaiah?" his companion inquired. "Are you listening to me?"

With an apologetic smile, Isaiah turned his attention to Yasmine. "Sorry. What were you saying?"

Yasmine shook her head as she lowered her menu. "I have to write this date down for the history books. Something other than work has grabbed your attention. I thought I'd never see the day."

Uncomfortable for having been caught, Isaiah flashed Yasmine a tight smile. "Pouring it on a bit thick, don't you think?"

"Hardly." She crossed her arms and stared at him. "We've been working together for what—six or seven years?"

He shrugged. "Something like that."

"And in that time, I've never seen you react to a woman like that—not even toward Cadence. I was beginning to think—"

"Don't you dare."

A wide smile crept across her delicate features. "What? A fine brother like you, a neat freak who loves the arts—I'm just saying it's highly suspect."

"Not funny. You just want someone to crawl into the closet with."

"No closet needed here. I blew the door off that sucker a long time ago." She eyed him. "Maybe I should wait here while you run after her."

"Not necessary."

"You need a woman."

He smiled. "And you need to stay out of my business."

"I tell you about my dates all the time."

His features turned into a comical deadpan. "I know."

She leaned over and swatted him on the arm. "Very funny. Be serious, will you? I worry about you. All work and no play make Isaiah a lonely man."

Isaiah laughed. "I date, Yasmine. I just don't have time for relationships."

Yasmine shook her head. "You don't wait for the right time for relationship. You make time."

The two friends held each other's gaze for a long moment before Isaiah nodded. "I'll make sure I keep that in mind."

She nodded. "You do that." She retrieved her

menu. "Now tell me why you missed our meeting with Mr. Alba."

Isaiah drew in a long breath and shook his head. "Let's just say today was not my day. It started when I was subjected to a rather thorough and intimate body search at the Bergstrom Airport. Then I landed at the JFK Airport and was told the airline had no idea how my luggage was routed to London."

Yasmine giggled. "My goodness."

"It gets better. Since I flew in casual clothes I had to shop for something suitable for our meeting. Problem is it's not easy finding something decent, ready to wear off the rack for a man my height. As soon as I could I rushed right over."

Yasmine looked at her watch. "Not bad. You were only two hours late."

"Was Mr. Alba upset?"

"Nah. I faked a call from you and told him you were late because your dog died."

"I don't own a dog."

"Then you shouldn't be too upset that it died."

"Yasmine."

"Come on, Isaiah. It worked. You know how crazy Alba is about animals. For a minute there I thought the man was tearing up."

Isaiah stared at her.

"I got us on his schedule for tomorrow afternoon. Everything is fine. So, order up, dinner is on me." She smiled.

He shook his head. "I don't know what I'm going to do about you."

"Hey." She waved her finger. "I saved your butt today. So show a little more appreciation, Superman."

He held up his hands in order to keep the peace and because she had a point. "I'm sorry. I apologize. Thank you, Yasmine, for saving my ungrateful butt. Can you ever forgive me?"

Her smile returned. "All right. Just remember we're a team."

"Got it." He picked up the menu. "Dinner is still on you?"

"Well, actually, I'm filing it on our business expenses. So eat up and enjoy."

Isaiah laughed and did just that.

He didn't arrive for check-in at the Marriott Marquis until ten o'clock. By the time he fell into bed, he'd reached a new plateau of exhaustion. But insomnia, his old and familiar friend, then chose to pay him a visit.

His mind roamed over the day's events and settled on the striking woman he'd seen in the restaurant. Was it her golden-hue complexion that made her stand out in a crowded room or was it her intriguingly warm cocoa-colored eyes that had captured his attention?

Isaiah drew in a deep breath and moaned as he exhaled. No doubt the fascinating beauty made some man happy. But what about the way she'd looked at him? Was it a harmless flirtation or an open invitation? He shook his head. What differ-

ence did it make? Their ships had already sailed
past one another.

Isaiah sat up in bed still clad in the suit he'd
purchased earlier. Now what? He still had his lap-
top. Maybe he should tackle some work. Lord
knew he had plenty to do. He shook his head. For
once in his life he wasn't in the mood for working.

He stretched and rotated his neck muscles.
Hadn't he read the hotel had a gym? Maybe what
he needed was a good four-mile run on the tread-
mill. Of course, any type of exercise would only
serve to get his blood and heart pumping, making
it that much harder for him to get to sleep.

Maybe all he needed was a hot shower. He
climbed out of bed and peeled off his clothes. By
the time he stood beneath the stream of hot water,
he had relaxed considerably. Fifteen minutes later,
he'd returned to bed. However, sleep continued
to elude him. Frustrated, Isaiah tore back the covers. He knew what he needed.

Brooklyn called her son, Jaleel, as soon as she
made it back to her hotel room. Of course, her
teenage son treated her as though the call was a
nuisance, but she ignored his behavior.

"What did you do today?" she asked, trying to
hide the dread in her voice. Whatever he and his
father did, she was sure she wasn't going to like
it.

"Dad let me test-drive a couple of motorcycles
down at the Harley Davidson dealership. It was re-

ally cool. Aunt Macy . . . I mean, Macy even took a few pictures of me riding them."

Brooklyn closed her eyes and counted to ten before she responded. "You know how I feel about motorcycles, Jaleel."

Her son sighed. "You don't like anything I do with Dad."

The retort stung mainly because it held a ring of truth. "You watch your mouth and put your father on the phone."

"He's not here right now," Jaleel said, his voice still absent of warmth.

"What do you mean he's not there? He's supposed to be watching you. Where is he?"

"At the hospital. They paged him in over an hour ago. Don't worry. I think at sixteen, I can tuck myself into bed."

This time she only counted to five. "I didn't mean to imply that you couldn't."

"Sure, Mom. Is there anything else?"

She didn't bother counting at all this time. "You better start watching your tone or I swear to goodness I'm going to crawl through this phone."

He didn't answer.

Brooklyn shook her head. When was she going to learn that getting angry with Jaleel wasn't going to get her anywhere? "Well, tell your father I'll call him tomorrow."

"Fine."

"Jaleel?"

"Yeah, Mom?"

I love you. "I'll talk to you tomorrow, too."

"Okay." He hung up.

Brooklyn held the phone.

Toni exited the bathroom wearing one of the hotel's large terry-cloth robes. She stopped in her tracks when she looked at Brooklyn. "How did it go?"

"It went like it always does." Brooklyn exhaled and hung up the phone. "I just don't know what to do anymore. We keep rubbing each other the wrong way."

Toni waved her off. "Don't let it get to you. He's a teenager."

"He's an angry teenager."

"What teenager isn't?"

Brooklyn smiled, but her heart remained heavy. "I just don't get it. Evan cheated on me. He left our marriage and Jaleel treats me as though it's my fault. Evan gets to enjoy Jaleel's laughter while I get his anger. It's just not fair."

Toni moved over to Brooklyn's bed and draped a supportive arm around her. "I know it doesn't look like it right now, but I'm sure everything is going to work out."

Brooklyn laid her head against Toni's shoulder, tired of searching for the light at the end of the tunnel.

"Why don't you get ready for bed? We have a full day of shopping and plays ahead of us tomorrow."

"You know what?" Brooklyn said, drawing herself up and standing from the bed.

"What?" Toni eyed her suspiciously.

"I think I need a drink. I'm going to the Atrium Lounge."

"You want me to come with you?"

"Nah. I think I need some time alone to think."

"Come on, Brooklyn. This is supposed to be a fun trip. There's plenty of time to think about our problems when we get back to Atlanta."

"I'll just have one drink."

Toni jabbed her hands to her hip.

"Just one drink. I swear after that I'll put all my problems behind me until we return home."

Toni held her gaze. "You promise?"

"Scout's honor."

"You were never a Girl Scout."

Brooklyn smiled. "A small technicality."

Toni laughed and gave in. "Okay. Go ahead and have your one drink. And tomorrow not a peep out of you about Jaleel or Evan—or Macy."

"Deal." Brooklyn turned and snatched her purse off the bed and left the suite.

TWO

The moment Brooklyn entered the Atrium Lounge, she felt out of place. It wasn't that the music was too loud or that the place was over-crowded. It was simply that she couldn't remember the last time she'd been to a bar. Could it have been as far back as college?

Maybe Maria was right. Maybe she'd turned into a prude. She frowned and removed the clip from her hair and shook it to tumble about her shoulders. Brooklyn D. Douglas was no prude.

"Good evening, miss. What can I get you?"

Brooklyn looked up at the bartender's friendly face. "I'll have an apple margarita."

"Excellent choice. I happen to make a mean one."

She flashed him a smile. "Don't hurt me now."

"If the lady will allow me, I'd like to put her drink on my tab," a smooth baritone floated from behind her.

Brooklyn's protest crested her tongue as she turned around, but the words vanished when her gaze met a familiar pair of gray eyes.

The man smiled. "Mind if I join you?"

The voice inside Brooklyn's head finally spoke up and told her to close her mouth and stop staring. "Sure. If you'd like."

He chuckled and slid onto the bar stool next to her. "Imagine my surprise when I saw you walk through the door. I never thought our paths would cross again."

"Oh?" She played it cool.

"You do remember me from the Broadway Joe Steakhouse tonight, don't you?"

How could she possibly forget? "Oh, yeah. I remember now."

He eyed her with a lopsided grin.

"One apple margarita," the bartender announced, placing her drink on top of the lounge's logo napkin.

"Thank you."

"No ring," the man said from beside her. "That's a good sign."

She glanced at his hand. "You're not wearing one either." Her gaze lifted to his handsome features. "Or is it in your pocket?"

He laughed. The flash of his white smile made him more stunning.

"I promise you. I'm not married—never been married."

"Well, I can't say the same."

"Oh?" He took a sip of his own drink. "A good experience, I hope."

Brooklyn shrugged. What the hell? "It didn't exactly leave a sweet taste in my mouth."

His gaze lowered to her lips. "What a shame."

A sweltering heat wave consumed her. "Why is that? Are you looking for a wife?"

"Not tonight." His gaze leveled with hers.

Brooklyn reveled in a pleasure that traveled clear down to her toes. The man's eyes cast her under a hypnotic spell—one she wasn't too sure she wanted to break. "So, what brings you to New York?" she managed to ask. "Business or pleasure?"

He took another gulp of his drink. "Business, though I can make time for pleasure."

She glanced down at her drink, convinced she was blushing like a silly schoolgirl. She was well out of practice when it came to the game of flirting. "How come I get the feeling you do this all the time?" she asked.

"Do what?"

"Pick up women at bars—or are you going to tell me that you don't do this often and there's just something about me that draws you to me?"

"*Now* who sounds experienced at this?"

Brooklyn laughed. "Far from it." She sipped her drink, and then glowed with surprise.

The bartender appeared and beamed a wide smile at her. "I take it you like it?"

"This is great."

"I told you," he said with a wink and then waltzed off.

"So what about you?" Her mysterious companion brought her attention back to him—not that it had ever strayed too far.

She glanced at him. "What about me?"

"Are you here for business or pleasure?"

She thrust up her chin. "Pleasure."

His brows rose. "Anything I can help you with?"

"You're rather direct."

"I meant whether I could escort you around the city, take you to a few plays. That sort of thing."

"Sure you did."

"Ow." He laughed with his hand placed over his heart. "I think you just insulted me. Don't I look the part of a gentleman?"

In truth, he did look the part. She shrugged and pretended her apology was forced. "I'm sorry. I didn't mean to question your character. I'm sure you're quite the gentleman. Just as I'm sure you don't make it a habit to pick up strange women in bars."

His laughter infected her. "What can I say? You're just going to have to take my word. But I do think we need to back up a couple of steps and allow me to introduce myself." He held out his hand. "My name is Isaiah Washington."

"Brooklyn."

His brows rose again. "No last name?"

"Just Brooklyn . . . for now."

"Well, I'm pleased to meet you, Brooklyn. What an interesting name."

"Not as interesting as my middle name."

"Surely you're not going to leave it at that."

She laughed and shook her head. "Believe it or not, it's Dodgers."

His features turned cautious before his lips slanted. "You're pulling my leg."

"I wish I was, but I have a father who's a huge baseball fan."

"So he named you after a baseball team?"

Brooklyn shrugged. "What can I say? They thought it would be cute."

"Boy, I bet kids teased you growing up."

"Nah," she said, laughing. "I told people that the D stood for Diane."

"Any siblings?"

"Nope." She thrust up her chin. "I'm an only child."

"Uh-oh." He clenched his teeth in mock horror. "I hate to do it, but I'm going to have to deduct one point for that one."

"Why?" She blinked, but continued laughing.

Isaiah shook his head. "An only child is usually high maintenance."

Brooklyn jabbed both hands to her hips. "What?"

His hands went up in surrender. "Sorry, but it's true. An only child is used to being the center of attention and can even be a little selfish at times."

Her mouth dropped open. "And exactly what do you base this malarkey on?"

"Experience."

She folded her arms across her chest. "Experience?" she asked with disbelief and shock.

"Yep." He took another gulp of his drink, and

then slid his cool gray eyes in her direction. "I'm an only child, too."

At another flash of his smile, Brooklyn's annoyance evaporated. "You had me going there for a minute." She waved a finger at him. "You're very funny."

"Ooh. I was aiming for charming."

"You're that, too."

"In that case, let me buy you another drink."

Brooklyn glanced down at her glass, surprised to see she'd finished it.

"Would the lady like to have another?" the smiling bartender asked.

Brooklyn's promise to Toni echoed hauntingly in her ear, but she dismissed it. She'd come down to mope about her problems but instead had forgotten about them. Which was easy to do when you had someone as handsome as Isaiah Washington sitting next to you.

He placed his elbows onto the bar and leaned in her direction. "How about the lady trying something different?"

Her gaze bounced between the two men. "Nothing hard. I'm not a hard drinker."

"I think the apple margarita gave that away," Isaiah said with a laugh, and then ordered from the bartender. "Let's see if she'll like a Scooby Snack."

"One Scooby Snack coming up."

"What the heck is a Scooby Snack?"

"If I tell you it would spoil the surprise. Trust me. You'll like it."

Her gaze lingered on him for a moment longer. "All right. I'll give it a try."

"Good."

Brooklyn took a long assessing look at Isaiah. "So how is it that you've been able to avoid the temptation of marriage?"

Isaiah gave her his full attention.

"First of all, I don't know whether I would use the word 'temptation.' Second, maybe in a way I am married."

"Oh?" she asked, hoping she'd done a good job of masking her disappointment. "You have a girl-friend or a live-in love?"

"Sort of. I'm, in an odd sort of way, married to my work."

Brooklyn nodded slowly. "I see. And what kind of work do you do?"

"Sales and marketing."

"So you're a regular suit man. I can see that."

"Oh, can you?"

"Yep." She bobbed her head. "Of course I saw you this evening, remember?"

"One Scooby Snack." The bartender returned and placed her second drink in front of her. "Enjoy."

"Now what is this?" she asked Isaiah.

"Come on. Where is your sense of adventure? Just taste it."

Brooklyn frowned. It was the second time her "sense of adventure" had been questioned. She grabbed the drink and took a brave gulp, and then blinked in surprise. "This is good."

"I told you you'd like it."

"No one likes a braggart." She smiled at his rumble of laughter.

"I'll make sure I keep that in mind." His gaze locked on her. "Do you mind if I ask you a question?"

"I haven't so far," she said.

"Why are you here?"

"Came to see a few plays with some girlfriends. We usually make this trip every year. New York is at its best during the holidays."

Isaiah's smile turned seductive. "That's not what I meant."

She frowned. "Then what did you mean?"

"Well." He looked at his watch. "It's one A.M. and I don't see any of your friends with you."

"Oh . . . that." She rolled her eyes.

He nodded. "Oh . . . that," he mimicked.

"Let's just say that I needed some time to myself."

"Did I mess up your plans?"

"No." She took another sip of her drink. "You improved them."

Isaiah's lips twitched with a blooming smile. "Glad that I could help."

Brooklyn suddenly became aware of the increasing amount of butterflies in the pit of her stomach. Their fluttering wings, combined with the warm rush of alcohol, gave her a delicious tingle. She drew in a deep breath and slowly licked her lips.

"Are you okay?" he asked, leaning toward her.

She drew in his scent and smiled. He wore no cologne or heavy aftershave—just the clean scent of soap. "You smell good."

His brows rose high over his eyes. "You don't smell bad yourself."

She giggled. She actually giggled.

"I think you've had enough to drink," he concluded with a soft chuckle.

Brooklyn bobbed her head, but continued to enjoy the wonderful wave of emotion flowing through her. "I was supposed to have only one drink," she informed him. "I have a low tolerance level."

"You're drunk off one Scooby Snack? I didn't think that was possible."

"Don't forget the margarita. Besides, I'm not drunk," she clarified, holding up a finger. "I'm just a little buzzed."

"Good." He inched closer. "Because I would hate for this night to end so soon."

She moved closer. "That would make two of us."

His slow gaze was like a lover's caress as it slid over her. "You're a very beautiful woman."

Every inch of Brooklyn's body warmed beneath the intensity of his gaze. "Thank you." She lifted her drink, grateful that it remained steady despite her nervousness.

"How long are you in town?" Isaiah asked.

"Just for the weekend," she replied smoothly.

"That makes two of us. How about I take you to lunch or dinner tomorrow?"

She moaned and shook her head. "Sorry. I have plans."

He smiled but disappointment flickered in his eyes. "Too bad."

Her head started to clear when reality threatened to overtake her. Hadn't she told the girls just that evening that she had no room for a relationship in her life?

Noel's voice floated back to her. *Haven't you ever heard of baby steps?*

Brooklyn controlled her shock at the direction her thoughts had turned, but Pandora's box had been opened and damn if she would close it.

"So I guess all we have is tonight?" Isaiah asked as he lifted a glass to her.

Baby steps.

"I guess so," she answered in a low whisper. Damn, he was good looking. When was the last time she'd been around someone who'd made her feel like a woman—a desirable woman?

She took a deep breath and lifted her glass to him. "Since tonight is all we have, why don't we spend what's left of it up in your suite?"

Three

Isaiah choked. "Come again?" he asked, swiveling his startled gaze to focus on Brooklyn.

Her chocolate-colored eyes danced as she leaned in close. "Take me to your suite."

Fighting his caveman urges to sling her over his shoulder and rush back to his dwelling, Isaiah instead tossed back the rest of his drink and tried to remain cool.

"Is there a problem?" she inquired with raised brows, while a ghostlike smile hugged her lips.

He blinked at her boldness. This woman was full of surprises. "My suite?" he asked for clarification. This was not the time for misunderstandings.

She nodded and moved even closer. "Your suite." Her full lips bloomed into another breathtaking smile.

His heart lurched and then its beat accelerated. No woman had a right to look like her. A man could lose his soul staring into those eyes . . . just as he was doing now.

"Are you sure?" he asked again. Slowly, her gaze

traveled over him and he belatedly became aware he was holding his breath.

She winked. "I'm positive."

"Then let's get out of here." Isaiah shot to his feet and jabbed his hands into his pockets. His fingers fumbled clumsily over his money clip before he was finally able to retrieve it. Depositing more than enough money to cover the tab, Isaiah caught a glimpse of the bartender's thumbs-up.

"Thank you and enjoy your evening," the bartender said, with a wink.

Isaiah had every intention to do just that.

Brooklyn stood up from her stool, laughing at his hurried motions. "You can slow down," she said in a low, seductive whisper against his ear. "I'm not going anywhere."

Isaiah hardened, but he was determined to behave like a gentleman. He gestured for her to take the lead.

"Thank you," she said, her voice lowering another seductive decibel.

As she stepped in front of him, Isaiah's gaze traveled down her back view. He drew in an impulsive breath. *Lord, have mercy.* The woman's ample behind was enough to make a man hurt himself. He lifted his eyes heavenward and mouthed, "Thank you."

When they reached the lounge's doors, he quickly stepped from behind her and opened it.

She flashed him another smile and Isaiah's arousal felt more like a steel rod pressed against his inner thigh. A soft romantic melody played throughout the hotel's grand lobby. Isaiah thought of it as a prelude to things to come.

Despite the late hour, there were still a lot of people milling about, but Isaiah had no trouble keeping his attention focused on the woman in front of him. She walked with the smooth, graceful gait of a runway model, while her hips twitched and bounced with enough seduction to make his mouth water.

When they reached the elevator bay, Brooklyn turned and caught him in the act of gaping at her assets.

She smiled. "See anything you like?"

Was she kidding? "On you, I like everything I see."

She eased closer, enchanting him further with her fragrance. "That makes two of us."

This woman was something else. "Where did you say you were from?"

She cocked her head with a slight frown. "Why?"

"Because they don't make women like you where I'm from."

She laughed, infecting him with its melodious sound. "I'm a Georgia peach." She placed a hand against his chest. "I hope you're hungry." Her gaze lowered to her hand and then traveled back up to his eyes. "Your heart is beating awfully fast."

He smirked. "Yeah? I'll give you one guess as to why."

An elevator arrived and both of their faces exploded with smiles.

"After you," he said.

"Bringing up the rear again?"

"Do you mind?"

She shook her head. "Not at all."

"Then the evening is already off to a good start."

Brooklyn laughed and turned to step onto the elevator.

Isaiah moved in behind her. He pushed the button for the forty-sixth floor and then turned toward her.

She gave him a come-hither look while her smile turned wicked as it slid into place.

Isaiah obeyed and backed her into a corner, fully aware that they could be seen in the glass compartment.

"Wait. Hold the elevator," a woman's voice boomed toward them a second before an arm bolted in between the closing doors.

Brooklyn and Isaiah sprang apart.

"Thank goodness we made it," a smiling woman said as she struggled inside with her arms loaded with shopping bags. "You girls come on," she called out into the hall.

Isaiah struggled to hide his annoyance.

There was a loud shuffling of feet and more rumbling of bags and then the small space was suddenly filled with six more women, all carrying bags by the armload.

"Are we all in here?" the director of the small group asked her companions.

The women bobbed their heads and released weary sighs.

"I'm on twenty-seven," one woman said.

"I'm thirty."

"Seventeen."

Isaiah moaned. It was going to take forever for them to reach his floor. He stiffened at the feel of a hand placed against his lower back. He glanced over at Brooklyn and she shared a look with him that made him forget about the women in front of them.

He inched closer and slid his arm around Brooklyn's waist. He smiled, loving the way she felt in his arms.

"Oh, look at them."

Isaiah and Brooklyn's attention jerked back to the other women in the elevator.

"Are you two newlyweds?" a perky blonde asked with a wistful expression.

Laughing, Isaiah opened his mouth to respond, but Brooklyn cut him off.

"Is it that obvious?" she asked, batting her lashes dramatically.

Isaiah's eyes widened as his gaze riveted back to the woman in his arms.

Brooklyn's hand roamed boldly down Isaiah's backside. "We can't seem to keep our hands off of each other."

The women took in a collective gasp and smiled warmly at the couple.

"Well, you do make an attractive couple."

"Thank you," Brooklyn said, without missing a beat. "A lot of our friends say the same thing." Her hand slipped down the waistband of Isaiah's slacks.

It took everything he had not to react to her playful antics, plus he wasn't at all sure he wasn't blushing in front of the crowd of gushing busybodies while they all smiled at them.

The elevator slowed to a gentle stop and when the doors slid open, two women stepped out while the other women waved and said their good nights.

Brooklyn's hand traveled farther south.

Isaiah decided it was time to even the playing field. When the doors closed again and the women returned to their idle chatter, he slipped his hand beneath the back of her blouse and glided along the line of her spinal cord.

She stiffened and her playful smile grew wider.

He found the clasp of her bra and skillfully unhooked it.

Brooklyn's smile vanished and astonishment dominated her features.

Chuckling, he leaned over and whispered, "Gotcha." He kissed her earlobe.

"Oh, just look at them," the one whom he'd overheard called Stephanie said. "I bet you two can't wait to make it up to your room."

The other women turned and smiled.

"How can you tell?" Isaiah said, grinning.

"Women can always spot an anxious man, honey," Stephanie said with a wave of her hand. "Trust me."

"Is that right?" He refused to hide his amusement.

The elevator stopped again and another woman

stepped out and made sure that she gave the "new-lyweds" an encouraging wink.

"Have fun, you two."

Isaiah nodded while his hand teased against Brooklyn's back. *God, she has soft skin.*

"Okay, you can stop," Brooklyn hissed and removed her hand from his pants.

"What's the matter?" he whispered back. "Can't stand the heat?" His hands skimmed the side of her breast.

Brooklyn's sharp inhalation only broadened his smile and caused his erection to throb.

Another woman exited the elevator and everyone went through the routine of well-wishes. Now, the occupants were Isaiah, Brooklyn, and Stephanie.

Isaiah couldn't be 100 percent sure, but he was certain the temperature escalated in the small compartment while he continued to exchange plastic smiles with the gawking woman. Wasn't this supposed to be New York City . . . a place where everyone made it their business to mind their own business?

"I remember my honeymoon," Stephanie finally said, her smile still hanging firmly in place. "We, too, chose New York. Mainly because, at that time, neither of us had ever been outside of Carson City."

Isaiah bobbed his head as though entertained by her ministry.

The elevator slowed.

"Well, I guess this is it. You two enjoy the rest of your honeymoon." The doors slid open and

Stephanie departed, managing an enthusiastic wave despite her armload of bags.

Isaiah patiently waited for the doors to close and when they did, he pivoted toward Brooklyn just as she grabbed the front of his shirt and jerked him toward her.

The crashing of their lips was like an explosion of passion, hunger, and desire. Their bodies rocked back against the elevator's glass wall.

Brooklyn couldn't believe what she was doing or what she was *going* to do. But when she experienced a prickle of doubt, her raging hormones came riding to the rescue. She had no time for a relationship in her life, but a night of hot, passionate, no-strings-attached sex, she could definitely make time for. *Baby steps.*

Neither realized they'd made it to Isaiah's floor, but a woman's loud gasp did jar them back to reality.

Isaiah and Brooklyn jerked apart. Embarrassed, they made their apologies to a startled elderly couple. He grabbed Brooklyn's hand and rushed out of the elevator.

Brooklyn couldn't stop giggling. She should be ashamed of her behavior, acting more like those blushing teenage girls her son dated than a mature adult, but damn if she couldn't help it. Meanwhile, a swarm of butterflies were attacking her from within. Could she really go through with this?

While the question echoed in her head, Isaiah

stopped in front of a door and pivoted toward her—the moment of truth.

When he smiled, in his eyes held a hint of caution fringed with a dash of hope. "I think I should ask you again. Are you sure you want to go through with this?"

Speech failed her while parts of her were suddenly at war with one another.

Isaiah tucked a lock of hair behind her ear and then gently caressed her face. "I'll understand if you want to change your mind."

His touch was like magic and when her gaze met his, she was lured into their hypnotic spell. A slow smile curled her lips and with her hand she stopped his gentle stroking to tell him, "I'm sure."

Four

Isaiah and Brooklyn tumbled into his suite, clawing at each other's clothing as though their lives depended on it. Brooklyn couldn't get enough of him as she gave in to a glorious and dangerous fire that nearly consumed her.

His shirt fell to the floor and her blouse soon joined it. Two quick kicks to the side freed Brooklyn of her black shoes, while Isaiah had to press against each heel with his big toe before being able to kick his shoes to the side.

He nuzzled her neck, which activated a switch in the core of her being; she couldn't turn back now.

Her bra slid off next and a wicked sense of pleasure coursed through her at his sudden gasp of amazement. Suddenly, his hands and mouth were everywhere.

Together, they fell back onto the bed, a mess of prying arms and seeking lips.

The man's touch was unlike anything she could remember; his lips were the answer to an unspoken prayer. Was the fact she hadn't been with a man for so long the reason he had such a profound effect on her, or was it possible this man alone had the power to awaken her body this way?

When his tongue taunted her nipples, her sudden gasp for air wasn't unlike a drowning victim surfacing for the first time. She ran her hands down the sinewy curves of his back, impressed by the strength they represented. Everything about Isaiah felt and tasted good.

His hard shaft pressed against her inner thigh and she had to rein in her raging emotions to ask one important question. "Do you have a condom?"

"Yes, I have some in my . . ." He stopped. "My bags." The same bags the airline lost. Isaiah felt sick.

He rolled off of her and dropped his head into his hands.

Brooklyn frowned and sat up. "Is there a problem?"

"Just a slight hiccup," he said. His mind scrambled for the nearest place he could purchase condoms. He slid a quick glance in her direction. "The airline lost my bags. You wouldn't happen to, uh, have any, would you?"

"Afraid not." Brooklyn struggled not to laugh at his childlike expression as he stared at her half-naked body as though his favorite toy had been taken away. "What about the convenience store downstairs? They must sell condoms. This is a hotel after all."

Isaiah jumped to his feet, conceding to her logic. He swiped his shirt from off the floor and, before rushing out of the room, returned his attention to her. "You'll still be here when I return, right?"

"After what I sampled, wild horses couldn't drag me away."

He rushed back over to the bed and extracted a long kiss. When he squeezed her breasts, she smacked his hand for his trouble.

"Go buy the condoms," she directed with a pointed finger. "While you're gone, I'm going to jump in the shower." She stood from the bed, but had to cover her breasts with her hands in order to recapture Isaiah's full attention.

He blinked and stared blankly at her before his brain finally kicked into gear. "Right. I'm going right now," he said, backing up. He started to button his shirt but discovered there were only three usable buttons left. He glanced back at Brooklyn.

She shrugged. "Sorry."

Laughing, he stole another kiss and rushed toward the door. "I'll be back in a few minutes."

"I'll be waiting," she promised and watched as the door closed behind him. Once alone, she expelled a long breath and fell back across the bed. "That man is incredible." She smiled and stretched along the rumpled sheets. She could still feel his hot hands and mouth roaming over her body—God, that mouth.

She laughed at the wicked memory, and then drew herself up to take her shower. The thought of leaving did cross her mind, a sort of no-harm, no-foul kind of a thing, but the truth was she was enjoying this side of herself. It was a side she'd long forgotten, but could embellish just this once.

Isaiah drew his fair share of stares as he made his way down to the first floor. And if he hadn't been in such a hurry, he would've had the mind to be more embarrassed about being barefoot, and wearing a shirt that looked like it had barely survived a battle with Godzilla. But as it was, when he rushed into the store and blurted out what he needed to the woman behind the counter, he heard a loud gasp and a few chuckles from behind him.

He turned and once again saw the elderly couple from the elevator.

"Lubricated or nonlubricated?"

"What?" Isaiah pivoted back toward the counter with his hackles at attention.

"The condoms?" the young and perky brunette asked, smiling up at him.

"Uh, lubricated," he answered in a low whisper and jabbed his hands into his pocket for money.

"Ribbed or extra sensitive?"

Was she kidding? "Just give me those." He pointed to a purple package and waited patiently for her to ring it up. Seconds later, he paid, waved off his change, and rushed out of the small store, but not without hearing a few more chuckles being made on his behalf.

Now, Isaiah focused on getting back upstairs

where he hoped to find his midnight angel with the baby-soft skin and delicious body.

When he entered his suite, he smiled at the sound of the shower running. His luck was still holding up. In a flash he tore out of his shirt and hurried over to the bed. Suddenly he didn't know how he wanted to do this. Should he go ahead and strip naked or should he wait and let her help him get undressed?

He thought about it for a full minute, and then laughed. When was the last time he'd been this anxious over a woman?

The shower stopped and Isaiah tossed the purple package onto the nightstand and dove onto the bed with the decision to just wing it. However, the seconds inched along at an incredibly slow pace, giving him enough time for yet another wave of anxiety. He rethought his positioning on the bed and draped himself across the pillows, but decided the pose made him appear too eager. Moving the pillows, he leaned back against the headboard, and then hated that pose as well.

The shower curtain slid over the rail. He needed to hurry and make a decision. Jumping to his feet, he warmed to the idea that he should be standing when she joined him. Standing and doing what? He looked around. A surge of inspiration hit when his eyes landed on the bar. Make the woman a drink. A sly smile slid across his face as he crossed the room.

This level of anxiety was like nothing he'd ever experienced before. He wanted to impress this woman—badly. The bathroom door swung open just as he reached the bar. Isaiah turned in its direction and was rendered speechless at the vision in front of him.

She had pinned her thick mane up in the back, but a few wet tendrils hung on the sides of her oval face. Her eyes appeared rounder, clearer, and they drew him toward her.

His eyes slid down her shoulders, hypnotized by the way they glistened beneath the bathroom lighting. The plush bath towel wrapped around her curvaceous figure fit like a custom-made designer dress.

"Were you about to make me a drink?" she asked in a husky whisper.

Isaiah caught the slight tremor in her voice and became concerned. "Do you need one?"

She drew in a deep breath and flashed him a fluttering smile. "Maybe just a small one."

He turned back to the bar and made two drinks. While he poured, he searched for other ways he could try to relax her. "The only thing we're missing now is some music," he joked.

"There's a radio clock on the nightstand," she suggested, stepping into the bedroom.

He grabbed their glasses and walked over to her.

Brooklyn accepted the glass. "Thank you."

Her hand brushed against his and currents of electricity surged between them. Isaiah couldn't explain the strange stirring in his blood—he was afraid to. "Are you nervous?"

She smiled. "Is it that obvious?"

"Actually, no." He chuckled before taking a sip of his drink. "I'm starting to have second thoughts about this being your first time for this sort of thing."

She shared a nervous laugh. "Trust me. It's a miracle my trembling legs are still holding me up." She, too, took a sip of her drink and immediately welcomed the warmth that rushed through her body.

"You know there's still time for you to back out of this," he informed her in a low whisper.

She met his intense gaze with a renewed determination. "Not on your life."

Isaiah reclaimed her glass and sat their drinks down on the nearby desk table, and then allowed his gaze to drink in her beauty. He noted absently that at each angle he discovered something new or fascinating about her features. How did he miss the small mole above her upper lip or the slight dimple in the center of her chin?

He reached up and trailed a finger along the side of her face. "Simply beautiful," he whispered.

Brooklyn watched his head's slow descent as he leaned in for a kiss. Every nerve in her body jittered and jumped with anticipation and at the feel of his soft lips pressed against her own, they ignited and exploded with emotion.

The towel fell to the floor and her body shivered from the room's cool temperature or perhaps it was just a reaction from his feathery touch. Their kiss ended and his lips deserted her mouth to burn a trail down the column of her neck. Weak-kneed, Brooklyn's insides were all aflutter. This slow seduction just might be her undoing.

She liked the way her head swam in a pool of euphoria and loved the feel of her breasts pressed against his muscled chest. Tilting her head back, she gave his exploring lips better access, while his magical fingers toured every curve of her body.

A glitch occurred in her memory; she couldn't recall when or how he'd placed her onto the bed, but there she was—submissive beneath him and ready to take the chance of a lifetime.

His smiling face hovered above her. "Last chance, but I swear, if you get up, you'll see a grown man cry."

Brooklyn continued to be impressed by his kindness. "Has anyone ever told you that you talk too much?"

He laughed and dipped his head low to extract a kiss. The man was addictive as any illegal drug. Everything about him overwhelmed her. In what seemed like forever, his lips and hands paid homage to every inch of her. She squirmed beneath his gentle suckling, drifting aimlessly on lofty clouds of heaven.

She ran her hands through his short hair, down his broad shoulders, and along the many dips and plains of his back, while she remained lost in a world that she'd long forgotten.

"You taste so good," he breathed huskily against

her ear, his struggle for control reflected in his voice.

"I want to taste you now," she said, slowly rolling onto her side, and then over still to take the top position. She copied his earlier moves by gently nibbling his neck, placing soft kisses along his collarbone, and finally gliding her tongue down to flick teasingly over his own hardened nipples.

She laughed when his body quivered beneath her.

"Girl, you're something else," he said with a rumble of laughter that filled the room.

"You ain't seen nothing yet." She eyed and reached for the condoms lying on the nightstand and read the box. "Orgasm control? Deluxe size?"

He rolled his eyes. "Please don't ask."

"Now, you've really got me curious. Let's see if I can get you out of these pants."

He helped her do just that and when he sat naked before her, all humor faded and her only response was, "Oh, my."

The control he exhibited while her silky hands slid on the condom was something for the record books. "Come here. I want to play with you some more first," he said, gently shifting her to lie beside him.

And play with her he did. Over a long while, he kissed, sucked, and worshiped her body in a way that may have been considered indecent to some, but was downright pleasurable to Brooklyn. Her hands gripped the bedcovers in a steel vise as her body soared with each mind-shattering orgasm.

Just when she thought she couldn't take any more, Isaiah entered her and stole her very breath. She was consumed by the fullness of him as he rocked smoothly inside her; each stroke drove her that much closer to the edge of oblivion. Shamelessly, her hips met his every thrust while her raspy moans mingled with his "Oh, Gods."

It was as if their bodies were making beautiful music together. Brooklyn could hear an orchestra building to a climactic crescendo in her head. In all her years of marriage, she'd never experienced rapture like this before.

Isaiah knew what heaven looked like, felt like, and tasted like. It was everything that was in his arms. He was certain of that much.

Slowly her arms slid around his back and her nails sank into his skin. He winced at the sweet pain, while his thrusts plunged deeper.

Brooklyn soared, reveling in the ecstasy and wonder he provided. She was lost in a turbulent whirlpool of emotion as she thrashed among the pillows. A fire lit in her intimate core and within seconds had built into an uncontrollable inferno. Isaiah must have been scorched by the flames, for his cry for relief matched her own.

The lovers' movements became frenzied as they raced toward an unseen finish line. A familiar sensation ebbed its way into her soul, then its violent eruption vibrated through her body.

Isaiah's grip on her waist tightened as his roar of release left him trembling.

However, it was just round one for the uninhibited lovers. As the night wore on, they experimented with different positions, some becoming an instant favorite with Brooklyn, others a favorite for Isaiah. But one thing was certainly clear for Brooklyn: she would never forget this night.

Five

Just before five A.M. Brooklyn stood by the window, wearing Isaiah's torn shirt and gazing at the bright lights of Times Square. The streets were alive with people and music. What she wouldn't give to prolong this night, to somehow thwart the sun from ever rising and delivering her back to the hell that was her life.

The sound of footsteps approaching from behind didn't startle her, neither did the pair of arms enfolding her, but the gentle kiss against her neck won a sly smile.

"What are you thinking about?" Isaiah asked, nuzzling her neck again. His hard, naked body pressed against her and reversed the course of her negative thoughts.

"How can a girl think with you around doing that?"

"Doing what?" He peeled back the shirt's collar in order to gain access to her sensitive shoulders.

She shivered with delight when an army of goose bumps marched up her spine. "I think the next time you do something like this, you should give the woman fair warning about your stamina."

His laughter was a low seductive rumble. "You should talk."

Brooklyn turned in his arms. "Let's just say that I have a strong competitive side."

"You'll get no complaints from me." He stole a kiss and when their lips withdrew, he studied her. "You never told me what you were thinking about."

Her smile fluttered weakly. "Actually, I was thinking about us and this night. I wish it would never end."

He kissed her again. "You know, it doesn't have to."

Her gaze shot up to his. His eyes were even more striking in the moonlight. A surge of regret hit her like a ton of steel bricks. "A relationship is not possible."

Disappointment chiseled its way into his handsome features, but it disappeared as he finally managed a crooked smile. "Nothing is impossible."

Resolving not to ruin what was left of their time together, she leaned up on her toes and slowly kissed each lid of his eyes, the tip of his nose, and then finally extracted a long mind-shattering kiss. "Are you up for another round?" she asked.

Isaiah's brows rose with surprise. "We keep this up and I'll have to run down for a new box of condoms."

Brooklyn laughed, and then allowed the shirt to slide from her shoulders.

"But we'll cross that bridge when we get to it." He laughed, swooped her up in his arms, and carried her back to bed.

At seven A.M. Brooklyn woke once again and found herself propped against Isaiah's muscled chest. She snuggled against him, content to lie beside him for as long as possible; but the morning light brought reality to her consciousness and tears to her eyes. And still she lay there.

Isaiah moaned in his sleep and draped an arm across her hip. She stared down at it, still amazed by how comfortable their bodies were together.

Gently, she turned in his arms and found herself within inches of Isaiah's sleeping face. Awed by his handsomeness, she smiled and then tried to etch each detail into memory. Lord, she wanted to stay.

But, it was impossible.

She reached up and tenderly traced her finger over his strong features and lingered at his lips. Why did it feel as if she were leaving a part of herself behind? It didn't make sense. She inched herself up on the bed and kissed him.

Despite being asleep, Isaiah kissed her back.

She waited a few minutes and then eased herself out of bed. The room was a mess. The bedspread, sheets, and pillows were sprawled across the floor, as well as the overturned lamp and discarded clothes.

Quietly, she gathered her things, while casting anxious glances over at the bed. Once dressed, she lingered at the door, staring at the sleeping Isaiah. In her hand, she held his torn shirt—a memento.

"Good-bye," she whispered and slipped out the door.

A few minutes later, Brooklyn returned to her floor and sneaked back to her own suite, praying she'd be able to enter beneath Toni's supersonic radar. In hindsight, she realized she should have called. The last thing she wanted was to have her friends worry over her whereabouts.

She eased into the room and breathed a sigh of relief at the sight of Toni snuggled comfortably in her bed. She tiptoed to her bags and stuffed the torn shirt inside. She grabbed a few personal items, and rushed into the bathroom for a shower. Once she was standing beneath the shower's steady stream, snapshots of her late-night rendezvous flashed behind her closed eyelids, evoking a delicious warmth throughout her body.

She ran her soapy hands across her shoulders and imagined they were Isaiah's strong fingers, gliding across her breasts and along her stomach. Her head tilted back in sweet torment. That man's mojo certainly had her caught up in a spell—one she wasn't sure she wanted to break.

"Are you planning to be in there all morning?"

Toni's voice boomed through the bathroom door, startling Brooklyn.

"I'll be out in a minute." She expelled a frustrated breath. She wasn't looking forward to going through the day with so little sleep, but last night was definitely worth whatever misery the day dished out.

She shut off the shower, wrapped herself in a towel, and hurried to open the bathroom door.

Toni stood with her arms folded across her chest. "Since when did you become so shy? Why did you lock the door?"

Brooklyn waved off her interrogation. "Sorry. I must have done it without thinking."

Minutes later, the two friends shared the bathroom mirror while they applied their makeup.

Toni frowned at her.

"What?" Brooklyn stopped coating her eyelashes in midstroke.

"You're humming."

Brooklyn shrugged. "Yeah, so?"

Toni stared at her friend's image in the mirror. "So, for the twenty-odd years that I've known you, the only time you hum in the morning is when . . ." Toni turned and nailed Brooklyn with an accusing stare. "What time did you come back from the bar last night?"

Brooklyn struggled to control her poker face and continued applying her mascara. "I don't know. I guess I left the bar around one-thirty." The truth was always best, she reasoned.

"Uh-huh." Toni settled her hands against her

hips, studied Brooklyn for a full minute, and then walked out to the bedroom. "You know," she called out over her shoulder, "I didn't think much of it when I got up, just figured you were being your normal neat-freak self, but your bed doesn't appear to have been slept in last night."

Damn Toni and her natural sleuth abilities. Brooklyn grabbed the hair dryer and proceeded to dry the ends of her wet hair.

Toni returned to her side. "Did you hear what I said?"

"What?" Brooklyn shouted over the loud noise.

Toni snatched the cord from out of the socket. "I *said* your bed doesn't look like it has been used."

Brooklyn's somber expression softened against her will, but she continued to put up a brave fight. "I'm trying to dry my hair."

Toni's mouth dropped open and formed a perfect circle. "Ohmigosh! Who? When? Why didn't you tell me?" Not waiting for an answer, Toni pivoted and raced back into the bedroom.

Brooklyn followed, a smile finally conquering her features.

Toni snatched up the phone.

"Who are you calling?" Brooklyn asked though she already knew the answer.

"Maria, you and Ashley need to get over here. You'll never guess what happened."

"Toni—"

"Brookie baby got laid." Toni squealed and plopped down on the edge of the bed.

Brooklyn tossed up her hands and fell back against her own bed.

"Okay, hurry. I think she's going to put up a fight on telling the details." Toni slammed the phone down and rushed over to Brooklyn with the giddiness of a six-year-old. "Tell me. Tell me. Tell me."

Brooklyn opened her mouth, but was interrupted by a loud and insistent banging at the door.

"Hold that thought!" Toni bounced off the bed and rushed to the door.

Seconds later, Brooklyn was completely surrounded by her girlfriends, who demanded to know every detail.

Isaiah's dreams of heavenly curves and ample bosoms had him moaning in his sleep. Despite being physically exhausted, his body still craved the delicious Georgia peach he'd enjoyed for most of the morning. His hand slid across the bed, instantly waking him when its search came up empty.

Bolting up, Isaiah's gaze swept the room. He bounded out of bed naked and raced over to the closed bathroom door. He drew in a deep breath and collected his thoughts before gently knocking. "Brooklyn?"

Silence greeted his ears and his heart plummeted as he suspected the worst. "Brooklyn?" He knocked again and turned the knob.

It was empty.

There was a knock at the door.

Isaiah sighed with relief. Maybe she'd just gone down to get some breakfast or returned to her room for a change of clothes. Certain of his conclusion, Isaiah opened his door and stepped back. "Welcome back to Paradise!"

"Paradise my ass." Yasmine rushed through the door like a hurricane. "We have less than an hour to get over to Mr. Alba's office. It's the only time slot available on his calendar." She stopped when she noticed the condition of the suite. "What in the hell happened in here?" Slowly, she turned back to face Isaiah and gasped.

His shock broken, Isaiah remembered his nakedness. "I was expecting someone else."

Yasmine slammed her eyes closed and turned around. "I can see that."

Embarrassed, Isaiah rushed to the bathroom, causing his colleague to jerk in a different direction when he mooned her. A few seconds later, he emerged dressed in a hotel robe. "Is there any way we can pretend the last few minutes didn't happen?"

Yasmine lowered her hands from her eyes. "And give up perfectly good blackmail material? Not on your life." She smiled. "Too bad I'm gay, you're carrying quite an impressive package."

Isaiah rolled his eyes while still managing to smile. "Back to business. What did you say about Mr. Alba?"

"Hold up. I want to know what the hell happened in this room last night. What did you do—have an all-night orgy party or what? This room is wrecked." Her gaze swept the bedding again, and she walked over to the nightstand, picked up the empty box of condoms and squealed. "Tell me everything!"

Isaiah moaned and shook his head. "No, no, and oh hell, no," he laughed. "I'm allowed a private life, you know."

She shrugged. "Yeah, but I've never known you to actually have one—even when you were in a relationship. Everyone knows that Isaiah Washington is all business."

"Speaking of which—about Mr. Alba?"

She drew in a loud breath and exhaled dramatically. "Fine. You need to get dressed. I have a car waiting for us downstairs. So, shake a leg."

Isaiah jumped into action by pulling clothes from his shopping bags, and then rushing to take a shower.

"And during our ride over to the office, I expect to hear the juicy tidbits of last night's escapade," Yasmine informed him, still smiling.

During his quick shower, Isaiah's mind kept wandering to Brooklyn. *Where did she go and is she ever coming back?*

A Wrong Turn in the Right Direction

Six

Six months later

Rotech's Golden Circle Award ceremony was being held in the lavish Embassy Suites in Austin, Texas. The guests were beautiful, distinguished, and successful. Many complimented and enjoyed the royal treatment Rotech provided while they congratulated and hobnobbed with the recipient for three years running, Isaiah Washington.

Isaiah smiled and shook hands like a seasoned politician. He said all the right things, made promises to the right people, and prayed for the night to end.

At a tap on his shoulder, he turned, expecting to participate in more small talk with another colleague, but when he faced Yasmine, he expelled a small sigh of relief. "God, am I glad it's just you," he said in a low for-her-ears-only whisper.

She laughed and handed him a drink. "Here. You look like you need this."

"Thanks. You don't happen to have an escape car running out front, would you?"

"Escape?" She shook her head.

He sipped his drink and a genuine smile appeared for the first time that evening.

"What?" Yasmine eyed him suspiciously.

Isaiah lifted his glass. "You brought me a Scooby Snack."

She shrugged. "Yeah. So?"

He shook his head. "Nothing. It just reminded me of something."

She dismissed his rambling and returned to the discussion of his desire to escape the party. "Sometimes, I swear you have a screw loose. Every year you slave for this award and then when you receive it, you act like it's a nuisance or something." She took a sip of her own drink. "I hear next year they're going to just cut to the chase and name the damn thing the Isaiah Washington Award."

His smile sloped downward. "Very funny."

"Congratulations, Isaiah," a male voice boomed from behind them.

Isaiah turned and nodded to his good friend Randall Morrison. "I see that you decided to show up."

"You know I'm always here for you, good buddy." He smiled. "Of course you know I still think you work too hard, but, hey, I love these parties." He winked, and then walked off.

Isaiah laughed and returned his attention to Yasmine. "I don't slave for an award. I just set out to be the best I can be, that's all. But when it comes to big social functions like this, I feel more like a spectacle than a success."

"Sorry, buddy. But you'll have to do much better than that to win sympathy from me. I'd give anything to have the career you're having. Everything you touch brings millions into the company. Forget Mike, I want to be like Isaiah."

He frowned. "Come on. You're on the fast track to the top. You could easily be the one winning this award next year." He took another sip and an image of Brooklyn flashed from his buried archives of memory.

"I don't believe in fairy tales, Isaiah," Yasmine continued. "We both know I'll never win that award—or have you failed to notice that only men win this award for a reason? Besides, I have too many strikes against me."

"Strikes?"

"Yeah. I'm black, I'm a woman, and I'm a lesbian. These things together aren't exactly what the company wants promoted next to their name in *Forbes.*"

"You're selling yourself and the company short," he said, frowning. "I hope this discontentment I hear in your voice doesn't mean you're thinking about leaving."

"Would you miss me?"

"Damn right I would." His entire demeanor turned serious. "I think you've come too far to throw in the towel now."

"We'll see." She sipped more of her drink and asked, "Did you see Cadence tonight?"

Isaiah grew uncomfortable with the sudden change in conversation. "You know Cadence and I are no longer together."

"That wasn't what I asked you."

"I saw her, but I didn't get a chance to speak with her, no."

Yasmine's brows jumped as amusement reflected in her eyes. "Well, heads up, because you're about to get that chance. She's heading in this direction."

Before Yasmine's warning sank in, Cadence's familiar voice spoke from behind him.

"Congratulations, Isaiah."

Isaiah's heart as well as his expression fell.

Yasmine took his drink. "I'll go get us a refill," she said with a wink. She glanced around Isaiah and smiled at Cadence. "Hello."

"Hello," Cadence responded.

Yasmine's attention returned to her partner and she added in a low whisper, "On second thought, I'll get you something a little stronger." She turned with a laugh and walked off.

"Aren't you going to turn around and talk to me?" Cadence asked.

With great reluctance, he turned with his politician's smile ready. "Good evening, Cadence."

Cadence, a breathtaking ebony beauty, smiled back at him. "You're not happy to see me."

Her usual directness made courtesy difficult. "I wouldn't say that."

She cocked her head. "Really. What would you say?"

Cornered, Isaiah fought his way out of the verbal combat. "I would say that I prefer not to see you."

She laughed, but her eyes flashed daggers. "All the more reason to see you."

Isaiah's rebuttal was cut off at the feel of his pager vibrating against his hip. He reached for it, but Cadence's taunt stopped him.

"Jeez. If you can't stop working tonight, then you're hopeless. Lord knows you never stopped working for me."

He left his pager at his side and leveled his gaze at her, but the hurt radiating in her eyes unarmed his anger.

"I've always been honest with you, Cadence," he said in a soft voice. "My work is my life."

For a brief moment, her entire demeanor changed and she mirrored the woman he'd met ten years ago. He took in her appearance, and noted that the strapless blue and white sequin dress was stunning against her willowy figure.

"Once upon a time I was convinced that I could make you love me," she said, lifting her chin. "But a girl can only wait so long."

This wasn't the time or place to be having this conversation, but Cadence always did things her way.

He moved closer in hopes of preventing being overheard. "I loved you, just not in the way that you wanted."

Her laugh somehow managed to feel like a slap. "Maybe you should have made that clear in the nine years we lived together."

He shook his head. "Selective memory is going to make this conversation impossible."

Her jawline hardened.

"Besides," he added, "opting to marry my sixty-three-year-old uncle is quite a consolation prize."

"He-e-ere's your drink," Yasmine exaggerated, rejoining them.

Isaiah turned and accepted the offered glass. "Thank you," he said. He turned back toward Cadence. "If you would excuse me." He placed a hand beneath Yasmine's elbow and proceeded to guide her along with him to the opposite end of the reception hall. "I swear if you ever leave me alone with her again, I'll skin your skinny hide."

"What? It wasn't a happy reunion?" she asked, amusement dripping from her words.

"I'm so glad I can be the source of your entertainment this evening." He glanced over his shoulder, relieved to see that he'd left just as his uncle took his position next to Cadence.

"Don't let them get to you," Yasmine instructed with a dismissive wave. "I'm sure the only reason Cadence came tonight is to try to get under your skin."

"Yeah, well, it's working." He took a deep gulp of his drink and relished the burn as it went down. His pager went off again. He frowned and retrieved it from his hip. He read the text message, blinked, and then reread it. "I have to go."

"Go?" Yasmine questioned, startled. "But the ceremony is about to beginning in a few minutes."

He turned to walk away.

"Wait." She grabbed him by the arm and stopped him. "What could be so important tonight of all nights?"

"It's my mother. She's had a stroke."

Seven

"Jaleel!" Brooklyn slammed her eyes closed and counted to ten. When she reopened them, her sixteen-year-old son stared back at her.

"You hollered for me?" he asked in a flat tone.

She continued on to count to twenty before stretching out a beautiful pink blouse. "Didn't I ask you to separate the clothes before washing them? I mean, I distinctly remember telling you five times this morning alone."

"I did separate them."

"Oh really?" She cocked her head. "Is that the reason this load of whites have mysteriously turned to pink, except for these three red shirts?"

He shrugged. "I must have overlooked them."

Had she not been up since the crack of dawn running errands for both the household and her business, she might have been in a better mood to handle this. But as it was now, she was running late to show a house located on the other side of town and the blouse she'd intended to wear had been ruined.

"Jaleel, *sweetheart*. You're going to have to start

paying attention to what you're doing. It's just the two of us here and I'm going to need you to help out more around the house."

Shoulders hunched, he sighed as he gave his usual response. "Yes, ma'am."

Brooklyn shook her head at his nonchalance while at the same time, she felt like crumbling to the floor and having herself a good cry—maybe later. She maneuvered around her son and, without another word, rushed to her bedroom to find something else to wear. As she passed the kitchen she noticed the dishes were still piled high in the sink, a chore she'd asked Jaleel to take care of last night and then again this morning.

Alone in her room, she slumped behind her closed bedroom door. "Lord, why me?" she asked. "Why does everything have to be a battle with him?"

Toni had suggested she call a friend of hers— some sort of family therapist. With each passing day, Brooklyn found herself warming to the idea. One thing was certain, something needed to be done—and soon.

In record time, she found a different suit and rushed out of the house, instructing her son for the third time to *clean* the kitchen. Once in the car, Brooklyn sped out of her driveway like a bat out of hell and when she reached the interstate, her car would've given any NASCAR driver a run for the money. Among friends, Brooklyn's heavy foot was often the subject of conversation. But for the most part, she considered herself a safe driver.

Well, she did receive two speeding tickets this year, but she was certain her investment in the small radar detector over her head would eliminate that problem in the future.

She glanced at the digital clock on the dashboard and moaned. A jet airplane wouldn't get her to her appointment on time, which seemed to be the norm lately. Brooklyn drew in a deep breath in hopes of calming her nerves, but that was better said than done.

Her cell phone rang and she feared it was her client inquiring about her whereabouts. On the second ring, she answered with an ebullience she didn't feel. "Brooklyn Douglas."

"Well, aren't you a burst of sunshine this morning."

Brooklyn's heart sank at the sound of her ex-husband's husky voice. "What do you want, Evan?"

"Just a few minutes of your time," he answered seriously. Actually, Evan was always serious—about everything. She guessed that he, too, was on his cell. In the background, she recognized the hospital's buzz of activity. He was in his natural habitat.

"All right. Talk. You have two minutes."

"Brooke, I didn't call to start a fight with you."

"Oh, no? Then I'll make sure that I write this day down in the record books."

He sighed heavily and then lowed his voice. "I just called to confirm that I'll be picking up Jaleel next Friday for the summer."

Relief and fear battled within her and she hesitated in her response.

"You're not thinking of backing out on me on this, are you?" His voice dipped to a hiss. "I swear, Brooke, if you do something to stop this, I'll drag your butt into court so fast it'll make your head spin."

"Don't threatened me, Evan," she hissed back. "I'm doing you a favor—considering."

Evan held the phone line and let his deep heavy breathing do the talking.

"Oh, my. Did I render the great doctor speechless?" she asked, smoothly changing out of the fast lane.

"I'm doing my best to get you your money." His tone remained harsh.

"Speaking of money, Evan, how can you afford this summer excursion anyway?"

"Jaleel and I need this trip, if for no other reason than to do some father-and-son bonding. It's just two weeks. The rest of the summer we'll be in town."

"He also has other needs—like eating and maintaining a roof over his head. You know, miscellaneous stuff like that."

"Five thousand a month is a lot of food, Brooke."

"We all make choices, my dear. And when you decided to sleep with my best friend, you made a bad one."

"Brooke—"

"Oops. Look at that. Your time is up."

"Brooklyn—"

"Pick your son up next Friday. Lord knows I need a break. He's becoming more like you every day." She ended the call and tried to erase all thoughts of Evan and her catastrophic situation, but that was impossible. Two minutes down the road, she changed the radio station, tired of the sexually explicit songs on the popular R&B stations. She landed on an oldies-but-goodies station as Stephanie Mills's powerful voice belted out a classic that mirrored her own deepest desires: "I need, I need, the comfort of a man."

"Ain't that the truth?" Brooklyn mumbled with a soft laugh. In her head, she was transported to a sweet memory where clear gray eyes worshiped her and arms of steel enfolded her. Where was the great Isaiah Washington now and did he ever think of her?

Isaiah finally landed at the Atlanta Hartsfield Airport after enduring a twelve-hour hassle of delayed flights and another overzealous strip search from the airport. Now that he'd reached his destination, he was able to focus his energy on getting to the hospital.

It was probably the thousandth time he'd cursed the distance separating him and his mother. He should have known something like this would eventually happen. His mother was getting older and he was her only child. Medical concerns should have always been a priority. It only made sense for him to move closer. Then again, with his constant traveling, it was still likely that he'd be out of town if something else happened. Around and around his thoughts and reasoning chased each other. Answers, however, eluded him.

Atlanta's summer humidity was a blow to his lungs and he found the heavy air hard to process. His white shirt and ironed jeans felt as though they were painted on. He dug around in his overnight bag and retrieved his shades. Now he was ready to roll.

Davidson's Luxury Cars met him at the airport and handed him the keys to a spanking-new silver Mercedes. Inside, it was equipped with an impressive navigation system. He punched in the hospital's address and in seconds had directions.

A large blue sign with a picture of a peach welcomed him to Atlanta.

"A Georgia peach," he whispered with a soft smile as he allowed his thoughts to conjure up an image of Brooklyn: the sweetest peach he'd ever known.

Suddenly, aware of the sea of brake lights in front of him, he, too, began to slow down. But then there was a loud crunch and his car jerked forward.

His gaze swung to the rearview mirror and back at the red car that had struck him. Great. Just what he needed. At this rate, he'd never make it to the hospital.

* * *

Brooklyn swore vehemently at her continued streak of bad luck as she veered her car off to the side of the road behind the silver Mercedes. Once they'd stopped, she heaved a depressed sigh as reality and the consequences of her reckless behavior sank in; two speeding tickets and a fender bender weren't going to win her any awards with her insurance company.

"I love my life," she mumbled with sarcasm and leaned over to the glove compartment to withdraw her insurance card. Next, she retrieved her purse and got out her driver's license. She reached for her cell phone to make the dreaded call to the police, but stopped when the door to the Mercedes opened and a tall man stepped out.

There was something familiar about the broad span of his shoulders that accelerated her heartbeat and thinned her breath. And when he turned to face her, she wasn't at all sure that she was awake.

Isaiah stepped toward the car, but when his gaze lifted to the driver, he stopped.

There had only been a few times in Brooklyn's life when she'd felt engulfed in a vortex of surrealism—discovering her father was Santa Claus, walking in on Evan and Macy in bed together, and watching Isaiah materialize right before her eyes.

"It can't be," she whispered and blinked, but when her eyes fluttered open again, Isaiah still stood staring back at her. Slowly, she reached for the door, utterly clueless as to what she was about to do or say.

For what seemed like eternity they simply stared at each other.

Isaiah regained his senses and moved closer to her car, but both asked in unison the question that was the foremost in their minds.

"What are you doing here?"

Brooklyn grew uncomfortable at the smile slowly blooming across Isaiah's face. Her surge of excitement was instantly at war with an equal surge of shock and dismay. Her gaze took in every detail of his features and compared them with what was already downloaded in her mind. Everything about him was just as she remembered.

Her brain declared each tingle coursing through her as a treasonous act of betrayal—including her accelerated heartbeat.

"I never thought I'd see you again," he said with an air of wonder.

She stepped back. "That was the plan," she answered before taking the time to censor her words.

He flinched as though she'd punched him. His steely-gray eyes held a level of caution. "That wasn't exactly the response I was hoping for."

Alarm coursed through her. "You came here looking for me?"

Isaiah frowned and stepped back as though he'd encountered a stranger. "You hit me, remember?"

She didn't have a response to that, but she still

couldn't let go of her suspicion. Brooklyn wasn't a gambler, but she was willing to bet that the odds of this bizarre meeting were a million to one.

"I don't understand," she said in a rush, her confusion refusing to let up.

"I don't either. Maybe it's fate?"

A red flag waved before her eyes and she determinedly shook her head to break the spell his beautiful eyes had cast upon her. "I've got to get out of here." She turned and jumped back into her car.

Perplexed, he rushed to the driver's side and leaned against the door as he spoke to her. "You're not thinking about leaving the scene of an accident?"

Her hand stalled on the ignition. That was exactly what she'd entertained for a brief and thoughtless moment.

"I would hate to have to sic the police on you, especially since I like you. But I will."

Brooklyn glared at him, not sure why she was so angry. Maybe because of all the men she could have selected for her one-night stand, she would pick the one that would boomerang.

"Speaking of police," she said, reaching for her cell phone again. "Shouldn't one of us call them?"

He nodded. "Good idea." Disappointment laced his voice as well as etched into his features.

Before she was able to dial the number, her phone rang. "Brooklyn Douglas," she answered. "Oh, Mr. Parris. Yes, I'm sorry, but I am running a little late. I seem to have gotten myself involved in a little fender bender."

Her client expressed rather harshly his disappointment for having his time wasted. She drew in a deep, steady breath and tried to placate him. "Yes, Mr. Parris, I understand and I do apologize. Perhaps we can reschedule for a later time. I'm certain you'll love this house."

He ranted some more, but she was relieved when he agreed to another meeting. She ended the call and breathed a sigh of relief.

"Brooklyn Douglas. At last I know your full name," Isaiah said.

"This has to be the worst day of my life." Brooklyn's eyes squinted against the bright sun and into his handsome face. Once again, her senses went haywire. It really was great to see him again.

"I'm sorry," she said, reaching for the door handle. Once out of the car, she flashed him a smile. "I'm being rude."

He held her gaze as if trying to judge her sincerity and then said, "Maybe you should go ahead and call the police. The sooner we handle this matter, the sooner we both can be on our way."

She frowned. "Didn't you hear me? I said that I was sorry."

"Then I accept your apology."

Their gazes held each other's and Brooklyn found herself wanting to repair the damage she'd caused. "I was rude."

"You've already apologized. Maybe I should

make the call," he surmised and turned toward his car.

Brooklyn wondered if there was any way she could crawl back in bed and start the day over again. "Isaiah—"

He stopped and allowed his shoulders to sag before turning back to face her. "Look, you made it perfectly clear by your words and actions that you don't want to have anything to do with me. I don't need a brick building to fall on my head. Let's just deal with this situation so we can get on with our lives. I have an emergency to get to."

She lifted her chin. "I told you in New York that a relationship was impossible."

"So you did. Foolish of me for expecting at least a good-bye."

A wave of shame caught Brooklyn off guard. *Who knew there was proper etiquette for one-night stands?* "Isaiah—"

Flashing blue and white lights stole her attention and simultaneously brought her back to reality. What did it matter the man's feelings were bruised? She hadn't lied to him.

In the minutes that followed, the couple gave their statements, presented their cards, and for the most part behaved as though they were strangers.

Brooklyn swallowed a lump of dread as she accepted the ticket for the cause of the accident. From behind the driver's wheel, she watched as Isaiah returned to his car.

The officer was the first to pull away from the

scene while Isaiah and Brooklyn simply stared at each other through the Mercedes's side mirror.

Isaiah knew he needed to go. His lingering on the side of the road was inexcusable, yet, at the same time, he couldn't understand the flutter of hope in his chest. For six months he'd prayed for the opportunity to see Brooklyn again and here she was—about to walk out of his life for the second time.

He started the car and took a deep breath. He would be the one to leave this time. If they were meant to be together, then their paths would cross again, right? Forcing himself to break eye contact, he pulled out of the emergency lane and merged into traffic, tossing his hopes for another chance with Brooklyn up to fate.

Eight

Brooklyn's day got worse. Mr. Parris was a no-show at their rescheduled appointment. There was nothing like a dose of her own medicine to ease the taste of her pride. She hadn't sold a house in almost two months and now she feared being able to make her own mortgage payment next month.

For a quick pick-me-up, she called the one person she knew could lift her spirits.

"Toni, can you meet me at Sammy's? I need a drink."

Concern edged Toni's voice. "This sounds serious."

"It's past serious and riding the line of critical."

At Sammy's, Toni's concern intensified as she stared at Brooklyn. "Okay. I'm all ears," she said, stabbing her salad.

Brooklyn drew in a deep breath while her brain flailed for a beginning to her story. "I ran into Isaiah today—literally."

The name didn't ring any bells for Toni and she

stared at her friend, expecting and needing more information.

"Isaiah," Brooklyn said again, shocked that her friend didn't catch on immediately. "From New York."

Recognition dawned on Toni and her eyes lit like the Macy's Christmas tree at Herald Square. "You're kidding me. How? When? Where? Are you going to sleep with him again?"

Brooklyn sighed and shook her head. "I rammed into him on the highway this morning— if you can believe it. And no. I'm not going to sleep with him again. The word *again* defies the definition of a one-night stand."

"A one-night stand was baby steps, remember? You're ready for the next step."

"The next step?"

Toni nodded and leaned in. "A fling. Not just any fling, but the toe-curling, skin-tingling kind."

Brooklyn recoiled despite being intrigued by her friend's blunt statement and despite her forthcoming protests. "I can't have a fling with that man," she hissed, glancing to ensure no one overheard them.

Toni laughed. "And why not? You already slept with him. A fling just means you continue to sleep with him. What's the big deal?"

"The big deal is . . ." Brooklyn drew in another breath, while struggling for the right words. "The big deal is . . ." She shook her head, unable to complete the sentence.

"Yes? I'm waiting," Toni said, cupping her ear.

"A fling is a notch below a relationship," Brooklyn finally managed to say.

"You're reaching into left field, don't you think?"

She didn't answer. Instead she stabbed her own fork into her salad as though the act would somehow alleviate her frustration. In truth, she did want to see Isaiah again.

"I don't know why he's here," Brooklyn mumbled.

"So find out."

"After the way I treated him this morning, I doubt I'm on the top of his Christmas list." Brooklyn moaned as she thought back to their chance encounter. "I was rude to him."

"So apologize."

Brooklyn met Toni's gaze. "Do you ever run out of answers?"

"I haven't yet. Do you ever run out of excuses?"

"I haven't yet."

The women laughed and continued to eat their meal of soup and salad. Whenever their gazes met, smiles fluttered weakly at their lips.

"Well?" Toni asked after a full fifteen minutes had passed.

Brooklyn gave her a farcical look of confusion.

"Are you going to find him?"

She shook her head. "Definitely not," she said with conviction. "Besides, I wouldn't know how." When she glanced up, she didn't like Toni's smug expression.

"Well, there's always the accident report."

"Are you sure your last name isn't Colombo?"

"There's also the Internet and your best friend, *c'est moi,* who has connections with people with questionable reputations."

"Should I be worrying about you?"

Toni shrugged off her concern. "It never hurts for a woman to have connections. You'll do good to remember that. I even think I know someone to set your ex-husband straight."

"Let's not forget Macy in this dream vendetta."

"Who's dreaming?" Toni laughed.

Brooklyn could only manage a butterfly smile. "I was pretty snotty to him."

"Then flash him your twin peaks and I bet he'll be willing to forget all about it. Trust me."

Brooklyn considered it. Not only was the man great looking, he was quite simply the best she'd ever had in bed.

Toni laughed. "Frankly, I don't think you have it in you."

Brooklyn rolled her eyes. "Please tell me you're not trying to dare me into having a fling. That's juvenile."

"Why not? We dared you into a one-night stand, didn't we?"

More crow pie, Brooklyn realized. "You know, I thought once you were an adult, you didn't have to put up with peer pressure."

Toni held up her hands. "What pressure? I'm just giving you some friendly advice. When you first returned from New York, you were a changed woman. You were singing and being optimistic about everything. Hell, even Evan and Jaleel weren't getting on your nerves."

Incredulous, Brooklyn's mouth rounded.

"What? It's true. Don't shoot the messenger."

"I've just been under a lot of stress."

"And sex is the best stress reliever."

Once again, Brooklyn fell silent, but secretly she agreed with her friend. Isaiah had performed wonders on her stress level. She did remember not being bothered by the news of Evan and Macy's outlandish behavior at one of their old friend's New Year's Eve parties. In fact her response had been "who cares?"

"Sex *is* a great stress reliever," she agreed.

"My point exactly," Toni said, smiling.

"Don't look at me like that. I didn't say I was going to do it. I mean, it takes two to tango and after what happened this morning, I seriously doubt—"

"More excuses." Toni shook her head. "If your night with him was half as good as you let on, then you'll have no trouble getting that man back into your bed. Trust me."

Brooklyn pondered the situation over again.

"Now what are you thinking about?" Toni asked.

"I wonder what was the emergency he had to get to this afternoon."

In a private room in Gwinnett Hospital, Isaiah sat beside his mother's bed, holding her hand as he waited for her to wake up. He'd never seen her look so vulnerable—so fragile. As much as he wanted to grab her and hold on to her, such an act looked as though it could break her. His lack of sleep in the past twenty-four hours took its toll and he could feel his eyelids grow heavy with each beep of the heart monitor.

When he'd first arrived, the seriousness of his mother's condition hit him like a ton of bricks and he'd vowed to start taking better care of her.

The doctor believed his mother would make a full recovery. It'd helped that she had always taken excellent care of her health, but the fact that she still had a stroke unnerved him.

Isaiah massaged his mother's knuckles with his thumb, trying to get used to the concept that for the first time in his life, he had to step into the role of being the nurturer. They were big shoes to fill and he was already feeling inept.

As he continued to sit there, his guilt held up a large mirror and he discovered a long list of reasons as to how and why he'd played a big part in what happened. Surely he could call more than twice a month, he could visit more than just on Thanksgiving.

In no time, Isaiah's eyes drifted closed and a kaleidoscope of memories and pictures filled his head. Within all that clutter, he couldn't find one snapshot of his mother crying or brooding. She was the kind of mother who had shouldered pressure and stress with a smile, and banished financial troubles with a dynamic show of ease. In fact, it wasn't until Isaiah prepared for college that he found out about their dire financial position.

Georgia Washington was quite simply the strongest woman Isaiah had ever known, and if anyone could survive this ordeal, it would be her.

Among the moving pictures of memory, Isaiah had trouble finding one of his father. He was killed by a drunk driver when Isaiah was four. However, his mother made sure to tell heroic stories of his father throughout his life. Melvin Washington was honest to a fault, loyal to those he called friend, and loving to all who loved him. Yes, Melvin Washington, a city bus driver, was every bit a hero—and a man Isaiah tried to emmulate.

Isaiah's head pitched forward, the falling sensation woke him up in an instant, and he jerked his head back erect. His gaze swept over to his mother and he was startled to see her smiling at him.

Georgia licked her lips and spoke slowly. "You look like hell."

Isaiah laughed. "Well, you've never looked more beautiful to me."

A weak chuckle escaped her ashen lips. "You should never lie to your mother." She winced.

Isaiah released his hold on her hand and stood up to reach for the pitcher of water beside the bed. "Here, let me pour you some water."

It took a few minutes to adjust the upper half of the hospital bed before he could hold the small plastic cup to her lips.

She took small sips and savored every drop. When she'd had enough, Isaiah removed the cup and busied himself with trying to make her as comfortable as possible.

The door swooshed open and Dr. Ramsey rushed in. "Ah, Sleeping Beauty has awakened," he joked.

Georgia laughed. "Paul, you're too young to be trying to turn an old lady's head," she rasped.

The doctor's laughter mingled with hers as he winked back. "Now, Georgie, you know how I feel about older women."

Isaiah frowned. Georgie? Older women? He glanced between the two obvious friends and judged the two to be very close in age.

"Maybe I should step out and leave you two alone," Isaiah joked.

They laughed.

"That won't be necessary," Dr. Ramsey assured him as he checked Georgia's vitals. "You gave us quite a scare."

"You know me. I always have to be the center of attention."

Isaiah stared at his mother. His mother was flirting—actually flirting.

When the two friends finished their playful teasing, everyone became serious and discussed the problem at hand. Dr. Ramsey spared them the doctor's square dance. Georgia's stroke was as quick as it was mysterious. Ramsey had no answers as to what might have induced it, which made him hesitate to prescribe or recommend anything other than rest and relaxation.

Georgia would stay a few days in the hospital for more test, but mainly for observation.

She nodded weakly, but her eyes still held a soft twinkle.

"Well, I guess I'll leave you so you can get some rest," Ramsey said, backing toward the door. "Mr. Washington, do you mind if I speak with you out in the hall for a few minutes?"

Isaiah glanced at his mother. Her exhaustion was clear as she'd already drifted back to sleep.

"Of course, Doctor." He leaned down and kissed his mother's forehead and whispered, "I'll be right back." He followed Ramsey out into the hallway. Once the room's door closed behind them, Ramsey turned toward him with a troubled look.

"I just want to speak with you for a few minutes—as your mother's friend and not her physician."

The statement surprised Isaiah, but he nodded, more than a little curious at what Ramsey had to say.

"Will you be staying in Atlanta long?"

Isaiah blinked, but nodded again. "As long as it takes. Why?"

"I think your mother would enjoy having you around for a while—more than the customary two-day Thanksgiving visit, that is."

The comment hit Isaiah like a Holyfield punch. "Has my mother said something to you?" he asked, trying his best to recover.

"Not in so many words. But personally, I think she misses you, despite having a wealth of friends. Sometimes there's nothing like having family around you—you know what I mean?"

Again Isaiah nodded and then flinched when the doctor slapped him hard on the shoulder.

"Good. I thought that you might." Ramsey pounded him on the back and then left him thoroughly chastised for neglecting his duties as a son.

Drawing in a deep breath, Isaiah turned to re-enter his mother's room.

"Isaiah?"

Surprised to hear his name being called from behind him, he stopped. "Yes?" His gaze landed on a beautiful blonde with twinkling green eyes.

"I don't believe it," she gushed, rushing over to him.

Recognition finally dawned on him and a broad smile came into place. "Macy Patterson, what are you doing here?"

Nine

Sunday morning church service was just what Brooklyn needed. Jaleel performed a beautiful solo with the choir, the preacher's sermon made her suspect her house had been wired, and Sister Loretha approached her again with promises that she'd found the perfect man for Brooklyn.

"Thanks, but no thanks," Brooklyn said in her kindest voice, but knew from experience Loretha would press the issue until she'd left to go home. Actually, this happened everywhere Brooklyn went. Everyone she knew seemed to hold the same belief that she was miserable without a man. Though she willingly admitted companionship would be nice and sex would be better, she wouldn't quite say that she was miserable without either.

"Sister Brooklyn." Freddie Wyatt, an old friend of Evan's, approached her with outstretched arms.

She turned as her smile struggled to appear through her stony expression. "Freddie." She allowed him to engulf her in his large embrace. He was known in the community as Big Freddie, mainly because he was just that—a six-foot-four-inch brother who easily tipped the scales at four hundred pounds. However, Brooklyn called him Big Trouble because that was what he loved to start.

"How have you been?" she asked, stepping back from his embrace, but somehow managing to keep a smile in place. "It's been a long time since I've seen you."

"You know me." He shrugged. "I can't complain."

Don't I wish that was true.

"You know I been meaning to tell you how deeply sorry I am about you and Evan's breakup. I can't imagine what could have gotten into that man, choosing some white girl over a fine sista like you. Tsk, tsk, tsk," he said, shaking his head.

Brooklyn should have been better prepared for that sucker punch. "Well, there's no sense in crying over spilled milk. What's done is done."

"I mean—I know Macy is fine and all, but still." He continued shaking his head. "Now, me personally, if I had been your man, I wouldn't dream of looking at another woman. You know what I'm saying?"

"I think I do." How she kept a straight face through his rude ramblings, she'd never know.

"How long have you guys been divorced now?" he asked, patting the sweat from his brow with a handkerchief.

She hesitated to answer, while silently praying that someone would come and rescue her. "Almost two years."

"Tsk, tsk, tsk. That's a lot of lonesome nights, especially for a fine sista like you. Are you already seeing someone?"

"Well—"

"I certainly hope not. A brotha like myself is looking to get in where he fits in, you know what I'm saying?"

She did laugh at that, she couldn't imagine him fitting into too many situations. "When I'm ready to date again, I'll definitely try to keep you in mind."

He dabbed his brows again. "All right now. I'm going to hold you to that."

That's what I'm afraid of.

Finally, Toni spotted her in trouble and managed to rescue her before Freddie actually hoodwinked her into a date.

It was no secret that Freddie and Toni were lifelong enemies, which was why Toni had no trouble telling Big Trouble to "get lost."

However, Brooklyn wished Toni could have been more tactful, especially since they were still in the Lord's house.

But Freddie was more than glad to sulk off.

"Why that pimp even bothers showing up here is beyond me."

"Do you mind? We're still in church."

Toni rolled her eyes, refusing to give up her irritation at the man. "What did he want anyway?"

"I'm not totally sure, but I think he was working up the nerve to ask me out."

It was a bad thing to confess, because Toni's anger peaked. "He's a pimp," she hissed.

"He also has those same connections in low

places you claim to have, and hence I try not to piss him off."

It was Toni's turn to remind Brooklyn where they were. After a few more minutes of hobnobbing, Brooklyn tracked her son down, and then drove them home. The car was as quiet as a mummy's tomb and layered with enough tension to choke an elephant.

"I spoke with your father yesterday," she said, deciding that it was time to end the silence war. "He's looking forward to you guys spending some time together."

Jaleel only nodded and continued to stare out the car's window.

She fought her instant annoyance at his behavior and tried to focus her attention on the road. The frustrating part to their strained relationship was that she was clueless to why he hated her so much and what he expected from her. But whatever this strange storm they were going through, she prayed it would end soon.

A few miles down the road, Jaleel turned toward her. "Did he say *when* he was coming to pick me up?"

She glanced at him, surprised that she had sparked his interest. "Friday."

"And I get to stay the *whole* summer?" he checked.

The hope in his eyes was like daggers piercing her heart. Was he that eager to get away from her? "Yeah." She turned back toward the road. "All summer."

* * *

Isaiah spent his days at the hospital. In the beginning he was more than a little hesitant to turn off his pager and cell phone. Thoughts of being needed at the office at any given moment or Yasmine needing help tugged at the back of his mind.

"I know I must be boring you with all this talk of my bridge partners and book club," Georgia said, smiling over at him.

"Nonsense," Isaiah assured her and meant it. "You run the Usher Board, play tennis three times a week, and even find time to volunteer at the shelter. There's no doubt in my mind on which side of the family I get my energy from."

She laughed. "My mother always told me that an idle mind was the devil's workshop, so I make sure that I stay busy."

Isaiah smiled at the instant memory of his grandma. "Nana used to tell me the same thing." He squeezed her hand when he noticed her faraway look. "I miss her, too."

Georgia wiped at a stray tear. "She was a strong woman—raised fourteen children by herself and a few of them weren't her own."

"She was something else," he added.

Her mother drew in a deep breath. "Let's talk about something else."

"Like what?"

"Like you," she said, returning the squeeze to his hand. "We hardly ever talk about you."

Isaiah continued to laugh, but he shifted in his chair uncomfortably. "Besides work, there's nothing really to talk about."

"How's the relationship between you and your uncle?"

"Strained."

She nodded. "I guess I can understand that—given the circumstances. But it's been a little while and family is family after all."

"I know," he said, lowering his gaze.

"Were you ever planning to marry Cadence?" his mother asked bluntly.

"Momma, I don't want to discuss this."

"You need to discuss it with someone. I think it's the only way you're going to be able to move on."

"I have moved on."

"Oh?" She perked up. "Are you finally seeing someone new?"

Georgia's face flashed at him and he hesitated. "No, not really."

She eyed him suspiciously. "You're not telling me something. I can always tell when you're trying to hide something."

"Much to my chagrin, but no. I met someone, but it was nothing."

"Sure doesn't look like nothing."

He nodded and shrugged with indifference. "Maybe the truth is I met a great woman, who doesn't want to have anything to do with me."

Ten

"You feel so good," Isaiah whispered against Brooklyn's ear.

Waves of passion crashed within her with each thrust. Her nails dug into his back as she tried to satisfy an insatiable hunger. "Please," she pleaded, gripping the smooth curve of his butt in a vain attempt to quicken his rhythm.

A pool of ecstasy swirled around her while she lifted her hips in wanton abandonment.

"Please, what?" he asked, nibbling her earlobes, and paying special attention to the sensitive areas of her neck.

Despite Isaiah's slow and deliberate tempo, a small blaze ignited, and in mere seconds, its intense flames licked her inner walls and consumed her in a raging inferno. Her nails sank deeper into his soft skin and she ignored his sharp intake of breath while she thrashed among the pillows. A strangled cry of pleasure tore from her lips and for a few heart-pounding seconds, she lay still until she gathered control of her ragged breathing and opened her eyes.

What greeted her wasn't the wide-open space of a Marriott suite, but instead the familiar décor of her own bedroom. As a reminder of what had transpired, her legs still trembled from the orgasmic relief she gave herself while lost in a sweet memory. A few seconds later, her alarm blared. It was time to start another grim and hectic Monday.

She rolled onto her side and hit the snooze button, and then snuggled back beneath the sheets as she contemplated taking the day off—which is what she thought about every Monday.

Thirty minutes later, she managed to pull herself out of bed and then survived a scalding-hot shower. Since school was out and she suspected it would be noon by the time Jaleel rolled out of bed, she made herself a solo breakfast consisting of an English muffin with jam and a cup of coffee. She didn't know what triggered her reminiscent mood, but there she was, thinking about another time when her mornings were filled with cooking for her small family and making sure everyone had what they needed to start their day. They were hectic times, but she loved and missed them.

As far back as she could remember, all Brooklyn ever wanted in life was to be a mother and wife. Maybe the desire stemmed from the admiration she had for her own mom. It was an admirable goal, she thought, and had convinced herself—which is why she felt no shame in not pursuing a career as many of her friends had done. What was the point? She'd had the good fortune of marrying a talented and ambitious oncologist, who went on to be a great provider and had allowed her to be a stay-at-home mom.

So what the hell happened?

Brooklyn drew in a deep breath, then sipped her coffee. "Life happened," she answered herself. She got caught putting all her eggs in one basket and watched helplessly when they all splattered across the cement floor of reality.

Dr. Evan McGinnis broke her heart. It was a damnable fact that she tried to get over every day. Her once-doting son became resentful when her undivided attention was obliterated and focused on her job. It wasn't easy becoming the first in her family to have been divorced—which was amazing within itself, considering the times in which they lived. But during *the worst thing that could have ever happened*, she found an independence she valued and vowed to never relinquish.

Once she'd finished breakfast, Brooklyn set about starting her day, but Monday wouldn't be Monday if it didn't start with bad news.

The phone rang as she made her way toward the front door. For a brief moment, she'd thought about letting the call go to the answering machine, but then thought better of it and turned around to answer it.

"Hello."

"Brooklyn, I'm glad I caught you," Cassandra Michaels, Brooklyn's attorney, said in a pinched voice.

Brooklyn's heart squeezed, certain that an unexpected call could be anything other than bad news. "Is there a problem?"

Cassandra's hesitation was answer enough for Brooklyn and she slowly lowered herself into the armchair next to the phone. "What is it?"

"I'm going to be in and out for most of the day. Is there any way you can meet me for drinks at Kelly's after hours this evening?"

"Can't you just tell me what it is?"

Cassandra's long exhalation was not a comforting sound. "We should talk face-to-face. Can you meet me?"

Yasmine reached Isaiah through the hospital telephone lines and he was immediately reprimanded for turning off his cell phone.

"There are people who are concerned for you and your mother's well-being, you know?" Yasmine scolded, not bothering to hide her rising irritation.

Isaiah was comforted at the sound of Yasmine's voice despite her obvious annoyance with him. Their relationship was an odd one, but it was one that he cherished. "I'm truly sorry, Yas. I wasn't thinking."

"I'll buy that excuse. So, what's going on? How is she doing?"

"Good. She's even surprising her doctors," he answered. "If I didn't know any better, I'd say she staged this whole thing just so she could get me over here for a visit."

"I told you that you needed to visit her more often."

"That you did," he said, nodding against the phone. "One of these days I'm going to listen to you."

She laughed. "That should be an interesting day."

"My thoughts exactly."

"Well," Yasmine said, taking a deep breath. "Pearls of wisdom: stop beating yourself up over this. I highly doubt your mother wants you to stop living your life so you can play baby-sitter, but you should carve out more time in your busy schedule for visits. Did I leave anything out?"

Isaiah smiled as he held the phone and relished the words he needed to hear. "No. I think you covered everything."

"Good. I should be in Atlanta in a couple of days. Before you start protesting, it's strictly business. I have a meeting with some of our people out of the Atlanta office."

"Convenient."

"Isn't it?"

Isaiah crossed his arms and leaned back against the counter. "And I guess you'll be needing a place to stay?"

"Know any place?"

"The company would be welcome," he said. "Thanks, Yas. You're the best."

"That's what you keep telling me."

"Speaking of business, you'll never guess who I ran into yesterday."

"All right. Why don't you spare me the guessing game and just tell me?"

"Macy Patterson."

"As in the chief executive officer of Cryotech?"

"The one and only. And not only that, she's invited me to dinner with her and her fiancé tonight."

"I'm impressed . . . and jealous. You've got to be the luckiest bastard this side of the western hemisphere. We've been trying to get a meeting with someone at that company for the past two years."

"I know. And get this—she's aware of the progress we've made on the cryogenetics implants and expressed an interest of partnering with Rotech."

"I hate you."

"I ain't got nothin' but love for you, baby." He laughed and looked at his watch. "I got to go. Make sure you give me a call the minute you land."

"You betcha."

Brooklyn stared openmouthed at Cassandra, unwilling to except what she'd just told her as fact. "What do you mean Evan is filing for bankruptcy? He's not broke."

Accustomed to Brooklyn's temper, Cassandra braced herself for the inevitable explosion. "All I can tell you is that he has filed chapter thirteen." She shrugged, and then tried to ease the pain by saying, "Frankly, I think this is just a ploy to get the courts to reduce his alimony and child support."

"Will it work?" Brooklyn balled her hands at her sides, confident that she wasn't going to like her response, and Cassandra's silence was worse than any answer she could have given. "I don't believe this!"

"Ms. Douglas, there isn't any reason to get worked up until we know more. He might be experiencing financial difficulties."

"And Elvis Presley is alive and well and living comfortably in St. Thomas. Evan just doesn't want to pay—end of story." She jumped up from the table.

Cassandra held up her hands as if to remind Brooklyn she was an innocent party to all of this. "If that's the case, the courts will find out. At most this ploy will only buy time."

"Time for what?" she asked in a near shout. "Time for him to come up with another way he can screw me?"

"Brooklyn, I understand your frustration. Really, I do. But I need for you to be calm. We will get to the bottom of this. Just give us a little time."

She took a deep breath, but her lungs exhaled a long stream of fury. "This isn't fair."

Cassandra, too, drew in a breath. "I know. And I'm doing my best to fix this for you." She stood. "You have my word."

Brooklyn clamped her mouth shut to prevent her angry retorts from tumbling out.

Their meeting ended with stiff handshakes, and

by the time Brooklyn made it to her car, she was engulfed by a rage as deep and as wide as any ocean. But the last thing she wanted to do was to go home and cry into her pillow. She was tired of playing the victim and it was time to pay a visit to her abuser.

Networking had always been vital to Isaiah's success as a businessman. And this business opportunity with Macy Patterson was one he could hardly ignore. It was to be a late dinner, giving him plenty of time to spend with his mother so he wouldn't leave feeling guilty.

But he did feel guilty.

He drove up the long spiraling driveway, impressed by the lavish landscape. He'd always suspected Macy Patterson was a high-maintenance kind of a woman, and what lay before him only confirmed his theory.

When he got out of the car and stood in the night's stillness, his senses were greeted with a bouquet of floral scents he couldn't differentiate. At his quick knock at the door, he was surprised to be greeted by an older, distinguished-looking African-American gentleman.

"Hello. You must be Isaiah Washington," the man said, stepping back and allowing him to enter.

"That would be me," Isaiah answered, stepping into an opulent foyer.

The gentleman closed the door and turned toward him with an extended hand. "Dr. Evan McGinnis, Macy's fiancé. It's a pleasure to make your acquaintance."

Isaiah hid his mild surprise behind a polite smile and accepted the offered hand. "It's a pleasure to meet you as well."

"Ah, I see you met the man of my dreams." Macy's lyrical voice floated lazily on a southern drawl toward the two men.

They turned and greeted her with smiles.

Dr. McGinnis moved to her side and gave her a quick peck on the cheek. "You look radiant," he praised.

Isaiah watched their tender exchange, but wasn't convinced their open show of affection was genuine.

Macy's cool green eyes turned and appraised Isaiah. He shifted uncomfortably beneath the weight of her stare. When she flashed him a quick smile, her piranha glint disappeared. "I hope you're hungry," she said.

"I did eat a little something at the hospital," he answered.

"Then you're a braver man than I," Evan joked with a boisterous laugh.

Isaiah didn't know why, but he didn't like this toothy character.

Macy, however, shared with him a businesslike smile. "How is your mother doing?"

"A lot better, I'm pleased to say."

"That's great news." She nodded firmly. "I'm

sure she appreciates you rushing to be with her. It speaks volumes for your character."

"Well, I don't know about that. I'm just a boy who loves his mother," he joked as his uneasiness grew without explanation.

"Tell you what," Evan jumped in. "Why don't we move our little get-together over to the bar and I can fix you something to drink? If you've spent the day at the hospital, I know you could use one."

Isaiah smiled and allowed them to lead him to a handsomely decorated study. Everything he passed oozed wealth and elegance and he couldn't help but wonder about Dr. McGinnis's specialty.

"What would you like?" Evan asked, taking his place behind the bar.

"Scotch on the rocks."

"I'll have the same," Macy ordered, easing beside Isaiah and searing him with a mischievous smile. "I hope this isn't too soon for us to start talking about business," she said.

"Not at all." Isaiah smiled, liking nothing more than to get down to business. "What exactly do you know about our latest developments at Rotech?"

"Not much. Just what has made it into print. But I can tell you it has a lot of people on our team excited and talking merger."

That was music to Isaiah's ears—just before there was a loud banging coming from somewhere in the house.

Macy perked up and tossed a questioning look at her fiancé.

"Now who on earth is that?" Evan set their drinks down in front of Macy and Evan, and then headed toward the foyer.

Macy focused her attention back on Isaiah and did her best to pretend the ruckus wasn't getting louder, but all pretenses failed when a woman's voice thundered throughout the house.

Macy's expression fell as if struck with instant recognition. "I don't believe this," she swore, jumping down from the bar stool, and then rushing toward the explosion of voices.

Isaiah's curiosity was piqued as well as he, too, thought there was something vaguely familiar about the woman's voice. He left the bar and headed toward the now three screaming voices. However, he wasn't sure when he'd walked out of reality and into that strange dimension frequently called the Twilight Zone. But that was exactly what happened. It was the only thing that could explain why when he entered the foyer he was staring at a raging Brooklyn Douglas.

When Brooklyn's gaze landed on Isaiah, she stopped yelling in midsentence as her eyes bulged with shock. "Isaiah?"

Macy and Evan stopped screaming as well and their heads jerked from Brooklyn to Isaiah, and then back again.

"You two know each other?" they asked in unison.

Eleven

Brooklyn struggled to navigate her way through the shock that had entombed her body. This had to be some trick of the mind, some ill-placed fantasy clouding her perception of reality. But as the seconds ticked along, she realized Evan and Macy were still waiting for an answer to their question.

"Do you two know each other?" Macy asked again.

Suspicion and anger charged back into Brooklyn's expression. "What in the hell is going on here?" Her hands balled at her hips as her gaze swung back to Evan. "Is this some kind of a joke?"

Macy jumped in between Evan and Brooklyn, but looked uncomfortable for having made such a bold move. "I think it's time you left. We're entertaining a guest."

"I can see that." Brooklyn stepped forward so their faces were inches apart. "Now if you don't mind, I was talking to my ex-husband."

"Ex-husband?" Isaiah said, coming out of his trance.

Brooklyn's murderous gaze swiveled in his direction. "Like you didn't know."

He blinked, but confusion continued to cloud his features. "How could I have known?"

"Would either of you mind telling me how you know each other?" Macy demanded, settling her hands on her hips.

Isaiah supplied an answer while his eyes settled on Brooklyn. "We're . . . friends."

Brooklyn's chin lifted, daring him to say more. As she held his pewter stare, her body awakened with renewed yearning. Afraid her conflicting emotions were exposed, she deserted his gaze.

Evan pushed Macy out of the way and glared at Brooklyn. "What sort of friends?"

Brooklyn had trouble maintaining her anger while battling confusion and embarrassment. "How do you know my husband?" she asked Isaiah, ignoring Evan and uncertain she wanted an answer.

"Ex-husband," Macy corrected.

"And my ex-best friend," Brooklyn added as her gaze sliced toward Macy.

Isaiah frowned. "I don't think I understand what's going on," he said cautiously.

"That makes two of us," Brooklyn answered.

"Make it three," Macy chirped.

"Four," Evan said, unable to hide his irritation. "I'm still waiting to hear what sort of friend this man is to you."

Everyone's gaze raked him with that ridiculous question until he physically winced. "What? I have the right to know what type of company you keep while my impressionable son is under the same roof."

Brooklyn's temper exploded. "Don't talk to me about impressions, you two-timing, lying sack of—"

"Sh-h-h, Brooklyn. I still have a guest," Macy hissed, trying to regain control over the situation. "Can't we discuss this at another time?"

She glanced at Isaiah, her brain unable to absorb the fact he was there—in Evan and Macy's home. The scene reeked of scandal, but with nothing that made any sense. "Then I guess I'll just leave you to your *company*," she sneered, and then pivoted toward the door.

"Wait!" Isaiah received shocked glares from his host and hostess.

Brooklyn, however, snatched the door open and bolted through it as though the devil snapped at her heels. As she raced into the night, a cool breeze kissed and erased the dewy tracks of her tears. The emotional roller coaster had knocked the wind out of her and she needed to go somewhere so she could think.

Her name floated on the air, but she couldn't squelch the desire to flee. She jerked open her car door and jumped into the driver's seat.

Isaiah reached her and nearly lost his fingers when she slammed the door, and then cranked the engine.

"Brooklyn, talk to me. This isn't what you think," he yelled and tapped on the glass.

"You have no idea what I think," she shouted

back, and then slammed her foot down on the accelerator.

He jumped back in time to save his feet, but was left to stand in the darkness dumbstruck.

He turned his gaze toward the couple standing in the front door's threshold while they stared back as if he'd suddenly turned into a two-headed alien. It was perhaps the first time he couldn't rely on his politician's smile to get him out of a sticky situation.

Evan's earlier jovial features were now a stony mask of hatred. He stepped forward, but stopped when Macy's hand shot out to clutch his arm.

"Let me handle this," she said, and then rushed onto the porch and down the small set of stairs.

Isaiah braced himself.

When Macy stopped in front of him, she had no trouble putting on her best face. "Well," she said, smiling, "that was rather unexpected."

"That's putting it mildly," he said. His gaze cast over her shoulder and up at Evan. "I think your fiancé wants to kill me."

"Now *that's* putting it mildly," she agreed.

They exchanged polite smiles for the awkward humor.

"I should go," Isaiah announced, saving her the trouble of asking him.

"I'm sorry," she said, still smiling. "But perhaps that would be best."

Though he nodded, his head threatened to burst with questions he wanted to ask, but he knew he'd have to go elsewhere for answers. He turned in the direction of his car.

"I still have your card," Macy informed him. "Maybe I could give you a call and we can talk?"

Isaiah faced her again.

She shrugged. "My company is very interested in Rotech's vision. And I'd still like to discuss our interest." She shifted under his stare. "That is *if* you're still interested."

Isaiah's politician's smile rode to the rescue as he nodded. "I think we can handle that. Call me tomorrow. I know just the person you can talk to." With that he turned and walked over to his car. All the while, Evan's heavy stare followed him. It wasn't until Isaiah reached the highway that he began to breathe easier.

But the questions swirling inside his head wouldn't go away, and neither would the image of Brooklyn.

Brooklyn made it home mentally and emotionally exhausted. Parked in her driveway, she stared up at her house. It wasn't the sprawling mansion Evan lived in, but it was a nice two-story home centered in a nice subdivision that was the embodiment of the American dream. *What crap.*

"Come on, girl. Pull yourself together," she whispered, without conviction or motivation. She leaned back and laid her head against the headrest as she stared at the house.

The night's events had her at a loss for words.

Nothing made sense these days. Oh, how her world stopped when Isaiah walked into that foyer. Even now, she couldn't believe it. Was it fate or co-incidence that kept tossing this man back into her life? Looking back on the incident, she wasn't too sure that embarrassment and not anger was the reason she'd hightailed it out of there.

A light flicked on in Jaleel's room and she sighed with reservation. He was probably up wondering about her whereabouts. She gathered her things and got out of the car. When she entered the house, she was relieved to see that Jaleel had straightened up—that is until she made it to the kitchen.

What was it about that boy and dishes? A noise caught her ear and she stopped at the base of the stairs, but the house had gone silent again. Shrugging, she dismissed the sound and continued up the stairs. As she neared Jaleel's room, she caught shadows of movement from beneath the door seconds before the light clicked off.

Her hackles rose as curiosity dominated her thoughts. She crept toward his door and leaned in to hear what was happening on the other side.

A girl's muffled giggle flared Brooklyn's outrage and prompted her to burst into the room and flip on the light switch.

Jaleel sprang out of bed like a calico cat, dragging the top sheets with him to wrap around his naked body. His teenage girlfriend, Theresa, wasn't as fortunate. She was left trying to hide her nudity with her hands, and then with the limp pillows that were sprawled behind her.

Brooklyn fought to close her mouth, but instead a stream of profanity spewed forth.

Embarrassment and contrition colored the children's faces, and it wasn't until Brooklyn barked for them to "put some damn clothes on" that either bothered to dash for their garments.

Brooklyn stormed back down the stairs, clicking on lights as she went, and all the while grumbling, "I'm going to kill him. I'm going to kill him." She snatched up the cordless phone and jabbed the number from memory to Theresa's house and broke the heartbreaking news to the girl's shocked parents. By the time the two teenagers made it down the stairs and joined her in the living room, Brooklyn's anger had yet to cool.

Theresa's parents arrived in record time and escorted the sobbing teenager home.

When Brooklyn closed the door behind them and turned to face her son, she was indifferent to his mask of anger.

"Did you have to call her parents?" he asked.

Brooklyn crossed her arms and squared her shoulders as she glared back. "Let's get one thing straight," she said. "I am the parent and I don't answer to you. As of tonight you have lost my trust," she snapped.

"Dad wouldn't have called her parents," he challenged.

"You're not living with your dad."

"I will be in a few days," he sneered.

"Maybe I should change that."

Jaleel's smug expression fell. "You wouldn't."

Brooklyn lifted her chin and held her son's gaze. "I've been very tolerant of a lot of crap from you and I've had enough. Since you have made it clear that you couldn't care less about my feelings, maybe it's time I stop caring so much about yours. Go to your room."

She walked past him and headed toward the staircase.

"I'm not going to be able to stay with Dad this summer?" he asked again as though he hadn't heard a word she'd said.

Upstairs, she slammed her bedroom door before tears of frustration slid down her face.

Seconds later, Jaleel's door slammed too.

She hardly remembered undressing or sliding into the torn shirt she'd stolen from Isaiah in New York. For some strange reason, she drew comfort from it—even now. She slid into bed, but as she hugged her pillow tight, she couldn't help wishing she had someone to share her load. As she closed her eyes, a faded image of Isaiah drifted across her thoughts and a sigh of regret crested her lips.

Twelve

Brooklyn's head tossed in abandonment among her soft pillows, mistaking them for soft clouds of ecstasy when the alarm blared. Her hand flailed out and smashed the clock's off button. The memory of her true location seeped into her consciousness and an ache of disappointment filled her. She'd dreamed of being entangled in Isaiah's strong embrace again last night.

Last night, he'd worn a handsome, cream-colored ensemble that reeked of sophistication, class, and style. It had been the second time in a week she ran into him and the second time her body had committed mutiny against reason.

Sighing, she struggled to forget the way his eyes had softened as they focused on her, and how his voice caressed her skin like the smoothest of silks. The man had the strangest effect on her—to the point where she questioned her logic for pushing him away.

Then she remembered: she couldn't handle another heartbreak or another life-altering disappointment.

The phone rang. Groggily, she sat up and answered. "Hello."

"What's this about you not letting my son visit me this summer?" Evan demanded. "Does this have anything to do with that new boyfriend you've got stashed over there?"

Tuesday looked to be an echo of Monday, she thought as she peeled back the covers on her bed. "I see *your* son called you this morning."

"Damn it, Brooke. I'm not going to just sit by and let you ruin this summer for us."

"Don't threaten me. According to you and your team of attorneys you can't *afford* to have him with you this summer, or did you forget about your sudden bankruptcy?" At his long punctuated silence that trailed her question, she stood from her bed and shook her head.

"Evan, I'm not trying to be the enemy. I just want to be able to pay the bills around here. I'm tired of fighting—with you, with Macy, and even with Jaleel."

The silence over the phone stretched with unbearable tension before Evan's exhalation filled the line. "I'll bring you a check when I pick Jaleel up on Friday," he said.

Brooklyn leaned against the frame of the adjoining bathroom as a small level of triumph and relief rushed through her. "Thank you."

In the Gwinnett Hospital cafeteria, Yasmine couldn't stop laughing when Isaiah relayed the details of his business dinner with Macy Patterson and her fiancé. In fact, her hilarious reaction allowed him the ability to find the humor in what had happened—however small.

"You have to be pulling my leg," she said, wiping the corners of her eyes. "You must be making this stuff up."

"Truth is stranger than fiction."

"Apparently." She chuckled again, yet one glance at his fading smile and she struggled to become serious. "I'm sorry. It isn't funny."

He rolled his eyes and attempted to smile again, but the end result resembled a lopsided grin. "No. It's funny in a sad sort of way," he confessed, and then shrugged. "It's just . . ."

She studied him. "You really like this girl, don't you?"

He thought about it for a long moment and then hesitated to answer.

"Come on. You can tell me," she goaded. She slid her hands across the table and settled them atop his.

The corners of his mouth twitched as he nodded in reflection. "I'm intrigued with everything about her."

A broader smile bloomed across Yasmine's face.

Isaiah caught the twinkle in her eyes and groaned. "Don't give me that look," he said, easing down in his chair.

"What look? This is great news. It's the best news. We have to find this woman and tell her how you feel."

He held up a slender finger. "Problem: she's not interested in me."

She coiled back with a frown. "You don't know that."

"Don't I?" he countered. "Let's look at the facts: six months ago, she disappeared without a trace after the most incredible night of my life. Four days ago she rams into my car and then treated me as though I was the last person on earth she wanted to see. Then last night, she damn near ran me over trying to get away. None of these things leads me to believe she's interested in pursuing a relationship."

"Hmmph. Sounds to me like she doesn't know how to drive."

He laughed despite his deepening mood. "I have more important things to worry about than someone who . . ."

Yasmine watched him as she waited for him to finish his sentence. When it was apparent that he wouldn't, she attacked with a different angle of persuasion. "I've never known you to give up," she said in manufactured awe. "Especially when you want something."

The blunt challenge struck the bull's-eye of Isaiah's pride as his head bobbed in agreement. He wanted Brooklyn Douglas; there were no ifs, ands, or buts about it. But how he'd go about getting her, he hadn't a clue. "All right," he said. His mind scrambled for an idea. "I'm going to go for it."

Yasmine patted his hand and gave him a superior nod. "Good boy."

* * *

Wednesday morning, Brooklyn arrived at Conner's Realty, shocked to find her desk covered with long-stemmed roses. The other women in the office cast curious glances spiked with friendly jealousy. When she plucked the accompanying card from a plastic stem, it was hard for her to hide her shock.

—*Does the memory of New York keep you up at night?*

—*Isaiah*

She reread the card several times and then stared at the large crystal vases monopolizing her desk while a smile crept across her features. "Yes, it does."

On Thursday, a golden gift box with an elaborate red velvet bow sat in the middle of her desk. No one in the office saw who'd delivered it. With great trepidation, she unwrapped the box. She smiled when she withdrew a beautiful snow globe. She shook the small orb and watched the artificial snow swirl around a miniature image of New York. Also inside the box was Isaiah's business card and on the back was the instruction for her to call his cell phone.

She was tempted.

Later that day, Isaiah took his mother home. It was a great relief to see her back where she belonged. And she wasted no time trying to clean, cook, and dig in her garden, but at every turn, Isaiah was there insisting that she rest. So he was left to cook, clean, and heaven help him, dig in the garden.

Hoards of Georgia's friends came by to check up on her. A few of them dropped hints for Isaiah to meet either their daughters or granddaughters. He told them all that he wished he had the time. But any mention of him returning to Texas was accompanied by his mother's frown.

While running errands, he kept his cell phone nearby. When the last guest finally left, he rested a few minutes from the swirl of activity. "You have a lot of friends."

"A person can never have too many," she said, patting his hand.

Out of habit, he retrieved his cell phone from his hip and checked for messages.

"Don't tell me you're already eager to go back to work," she said, watching him.

He smiled and shook his head. "Believe it or not I haven't thought about work for a few days."

Disbelief covered her face as she waved off his comment. "That's like saying Dr. King never had a dream."

Isaiah laughed and eased closer to her on the sofa. "Is there anything else I can get for you?"

Georgia smiled. "You rest now. You've been ripping and roaring all day. I'm getting tired just watching you."

"Thanks. You're a good mom." He eased back

into the chair, and then cocked his head onto her shoulder.

She chuckled and he enjoyed the melodious sound.

"Did she call today?" she asked.

His spirits dipped, but his resolve kicked in. "Not yet."

She laughed and continued to pat his hand. "Don't worry. She will."

He chuckled at her misplaced confidence. "How do you know?"

"Because she'd have to be crazy not to."

Jaleel lay across his bed and tossed a baseball into the air with one hand and then caught it in his gloved one. He'd often performed this routine when he needed to think or when he wanted to mentally separate from his parents. Today, he wanted and needed to do both. He was tired of being ignored and used by his parents, whether they meant to do it or not. *Why couldn't things go back to the way they used to be?*

He was also tired of being angry—with his parents, with Macy, and most of all with himself. Sneaking Theresa over after curfew had been a mistake. He wished he could talk with her, but since that night, her parents had grounded her from seeing him or even talking on the phone. The pain and embarrassment he'd caused his mother was unforgivable. The worst part was he had no explanation for why he couldn't apologize.

Instead, he'd antagonized her and undoubtedly made her cry.

Jaleel stopped tossing the ball as he felt his own tears surface and slide to the corners of his eyes. He didn't mean to hurt her. He just somehow always did.

This morning his mother wanted to discuss what had happened between him and Theresa and he had had the embarrassing chore of telling his mother he was no virgin. However, it was his first time attempting to have sex in their house. His honesty was rewarded with a flash of disappointment and disapproval. Then the discussion turned toward protection.

When he revealed his father had bought him a few boxes of condoms that he kept in his top drawer, he thought he'd win brownie points for having the foresight of discussing the matter with his dad, but instead his confiding with his dad hurt her. He would never learn the rules of divorce.

Frustration erupted in him. How much longer did he have to wait for both of them to come to their senses and get back together?

"No matter," Jaleel whispered, and then willed his tears to disappear. This summer he had a plan and, if things went the way he hoped, they would once again be one big happy family.

Thirteen

Rain accompanied the dawn of Friday morning to the great relief of Atlanta citizens and their dehydrated lawns. But this was no ordinary shower; the blinding sheets of rain held every potential of becoming a hazardous flood—a good enough excuse for Brooklyn to try and work from home.

Jaleel had surprised her by bolting out of bed at six A.M. instead of sticking to his customary noon hibernation. She woke up and fixed him a hearty breakfast, undoubtedly the last one he'd get for the summer, seeing how it was no secret that Macy couldn't cook.

By seven, Jaleel had dragged a large duffel bag into the living room and looked as though he was shipping out for war.

Brooklyn pretended her son's eagerness didn't bother her and even tried to convince herself she was looking forward to the summer break. In truth, she didn't want him to go.

Jaleel walked into the kitchen and stared in awe at the feast before him. "Are you expecting an army?" he asked. A smile split his lips.

Then she truly noticed the mountain of biscuits, pancakes, sausages, and eggs she'd prepared. There were bowls of grits, oatmeal, and gravy—and she'd also fried a pack of bacon.

"Okay," she said, nodding. "I might have gone a little overboard."

"Yeah. Just a little." He laughed and sat down at the table.

Brooklyn poured herself a cup of coffee and joined him. "So, I guess you're excited?"

"I suppose so." He shrugged, careful not to meet her stare as he piled food onto his plate.

An awkward tension cloaked mother and son while one tried not to ask too much and the other avoided straight answers.

"I want you to promise to call if you need me to come get you for any reason," she said.

"Yes, ma'am," he said, more on autopilot than anything else.

Brooklyn couldn't explain the wave of sadness and guilt or her undeniable fear of spending the summer alone. Trying to keep the conversation on safe ground, she thought it best to run down the items he needed. "Did you pack enough underwear?"

She laughed at the incredulous look he gave her. "Sorry. It's hard turning the mother thing on and off," she offered as an excuse.

He smiled and made her day.

An hour later, as she placed the dishes in the dishwasher, the doorbell rang.

Jaleel bounded down the stairs.

Brooklyn's heart sank. She dried her hands and went to join her son just as he opened the door.

"What are you doing with a tux?" she asked, pointing to the suit draped over his shoulder.

Evan walked through the door.

Jaleel shrugged, but a smile quirked his lips. "Dad rented it for their engagement party."

Brooklyn turned hard eyes toward Evan. "What engagement party?"

Yasmine popped up at Isaiah's mother's home some time after lunch and was bursting at the seams with news. "I finally met with Ms. Macy Patterson today for lunch," she announced, and then stopped in her tracks when she noticed Isaiah was wearing an apron.

"Don't say a word," he warned, and then waved for her to follow him into the kitchen.

"Never a camera around when you need one," she muttered, with suppressed laughter.

Once in the kitchen, he resumed slicing and dicing onions on a cutting board.

"I never knew you were handy in the kitchen." She grabbed a mitten and peeked inside the oven.

"There's a lot you don't know about me." He chuckled, turning away from the counter to stir the sauce on the stove. "Tell me about your meeting."

Yasmine laughed and closed the oven. "Businesswise it was a boon. Her company is practically salivating over the prospect of working with Rotech."

"That is good news." He nodded though it wasn't the information he wanted to discuss. He glanced at his best friend and waited with strained patience for her to continue.

Instead, Yasmine took her time helping him stir the sauces and sniff everything she came across.

"Well?" he finally asked.

"Well, what?"

"You two didn't talk about anything else?" he probed.

"Oh." Yasmine smiled slyly. "She did say something about her total embarrassment over what had happened the other night at dinner."

Isaiah waited—and waited—then asked, "Is that it?"

Yasmine laughed and slapped him on the shoulder. "Quite the eager beaver, aren't you, Romeo?"

"Why don't you stop playing around and just tell me what I want to know."

"At first it was kind of difficult getting information out of her, but after a couple of drinks, she loosened right up." She eased onto a stool next to the counter.

"And?"

"And, she was once your Juliet's best friend— that is until Macy stole her husband."

"She said that?"

"Not in so many words—but yeah. Frankly, I think these people need an all-expense-paid trip to the *Jerry Springer* show."

"That bad?"

Yasmine cocked her head as her eyes rolled upward. "You know, now that I think about it, you two have a few things in common. Her husband left her for her best friend and your girlfriend left you for your uncle. This would be like two rejects finding eternal bliss."

Isaiah's jaw dropped as surprise colored his eyes. "Rejects?"

She shrugged, and then laughed. "I just call it like I see it."

"Sticks and stones." Isaiah scraped the diced onions into the saucepan. As he talked, his grin slouched to one side. "What else did she say?"

"That she wasn't looking forward to playing baby-sitter to her fiancé's son all summer. According to her, she's not the motherly type. And after listening to her for the better part of the afternoon, I have no trouble believing that."

Isaiah tuned her out. "Son?" he repeated, unable to explain his flicker of surprise.

"Yep, so if this works out, you're looking at a prepackaged family," Yasmine informed him somberly.

Isaiah laughed. "Well, the way things are going, I don't think that's a real possibility. She hasn't called yet."

"Then call her."

He shook his head. "I don't think so. I'm bordering on harassment as it is."

"What? We've only sent flowers and a snow globe. What's a phone call—at least one, anyway?"

"I don't know," he said, shaking his head. "I'm starting to feel like I'm begging."

"You are begging." She met his stare with a serious expression.

"I never beg," he answered in equal measure.

Yasmine shrugged. "If you say so."

Friday night, Brooklyn had invited Toni over under the guise of a girls' night out. In secret, she held every intention of hosting her own pity party. When Toni entered the house and followed her to the kitchen, Brooklyn told her the news.

"What do you mean 'engaged'?" Toni questioned in the same deadpan voice that Brooklyn had used earlier with Evan.

Brooklyn could only manage a casual shrug of her shoulders. "That's what he said." She popped open a bottle of wine. "Drink?"

Shock lingered in Toni's expression. "Is that the strongest thing you have?"

"Unfortunately." She turned and opened a cabinet for the wineglasses. "Was that a yes or a no?" she asked before pouring.

"It's a yes." Toni plopped her purse down on the breakfast bar, and then eased onto a stool. "Engaged?"

Brooklyn nodded and filled the glasses to the rim before handing one to her friend. "The way I see it, the two snakes deserve each other."

Toni eyed her. "Have you been in that robe all day?"

"Didn't see a need to get dressed," Brooklyn answered with another shrug. "My life is going to hell in a handbasket anyway." She took a deep gulp.

Toni's glass halted midway to her lips as she studied Brooklyn again. "You're not still in love with him, are you?"

Brooklyn choked, but managed to get the wine down her throat; however, her eyes glossed and a severe cough plagued her for a few minutes afterward.

Toni's delicate brows rose with heightening interest. "Are you all right?"

"I'm f-fine." Brooklyn wasted no time pouring herself another glass.

"Good. I'm still waiting for an answer to my question."

Setting the bottle down, she placed both hands against the counter, imprisoned Toni's gaze, and leaned forward. "Let me be clear. I am absolutely, positively over Evan."

It was Toni's turn to shrug. "Then it's no big deal that he's getting married."

"Of course it's a big deal. He's getting married before I am—and to her!"

Toni leaned back. "I see."

"He doesn't deserve to find happiness first." Brooklyn's body deflated. She grabbed her wineglass and the bottle and shuffled out of the kitchen.

Toni stood and followed her to the living room. She stopped at the sight of so many flickering candles. "It looks like a shrine in here."

Brooklyn ignored the comment and dropped onto the sofa. "Life isn't fair."

"Whoever said that it was?" Toni asked, joining her. She gingerly eased out of her pumps, sighed with relief, and then turned her attention back to her depressed friend. "You're right. The two snakes deserve each other and whatever misery they bestow on one another."

The alcohol worked its magic and numbed Brooklyn's throbbing temples as well as the stabbing ache in her chest. "You're completely missing my point."

"What *is* your point?"

She worked her mouth, but her brain seemingly forgot the English language.

"Yeeess?" Toni took her first sip.

Brooklyn's body deflated again. "I don't know. I just feel this huge injustice. He has the great career, all our money, Jaleel's undying love and adoration, my best friend—"

Toni cleared her throat.

"My ex-best friend."

"Thank you."

A corner of Brooklyn's lips flickered upward, and then disappeared. "And now, he's racing down the aisle of happily-ever-after or at least happy until someone with a firmer ass comes along."

Toni popped her on the arm. "Stop it. There is absolutely nothing wrong with your ass."

A bark of laughter reverberated throughout

Brooklyn's body and she knew that she'd done the right thing by inviting Toni over.

"Look," Toni said, settling back against the fluffy pillows. "If anything, this should tell you that it's time to start searching for someone for yourself as well. The past is the past and there's nothing you can do to change any of it. But at least you've learned some valuable lessons."

Brooklyn acquiesced with a slow nod of her head.

"I say you call that hunk from New York and start your own torrid affair, relationship, whatever. All work and no play make Brooklyn a lonely woman."

Cocking a brow in the middle of her friend's motivational speech, Brooklyn turned toward Toni. "What about you?"

"What about me?"

"I mean, great sermon, but I don't see you exactly practicing what you preach, reverend. When was the last time you were out on a date?"

"What difference does that make? We're talking about you."

"You're being a hypocrite."

"I haven't transformed my living room to look like some holy sanctuary while pouring my sorrows into a bottle of wine."

Brooklyn swiveled her head and rolled her eyes heavenward. "Whatever."

Toni laughed as she leaned forward to set her glass down on the coffee table. "All right, if you must know, I went out with Brian Olson last night."

Curiosity tickled Brooklyn's brain as she glanced back at her friend.

Toni waved off her inquisitive stare and began providing answers before the questions were hurled. "He works with me at the firm. Brilliant attorney, lousy in bed."

"You slept with him?" Brooklyn turned toward her, wrapped in her friend's story.

A sly smile dominated Toni's features. "Now who's trying to be a hypocrite?"

Flustered, Brooklyn again didn't know what to say, but at Toni's laugh, she smiled again. "Well, at least mine wasn't lousy in bed," she said, sticking her tongue out.

"Which brings us back to my point." Toni reclaimed her glass. "Call Isaiah."

Fourteen

Entrenched in a horror movie's climax, Yasmine jumped when a loud shrill filled the room. She retrieved her cell phone, but it wasn't ringing. A phone continued to ring while she searched around her before finding Isaiah's cell phone buried between the cushions. She pressed the talk button. "Hello."

"Sorry. I must have the wrong number," a woman answered.

"No, wait—"

The lady disconnected the call. Yasmine frowned at the phone just as Isaiah returned from the twenty-four-hour pharmacy.

When he breezed through the front door, he stopped by the living room. "Yas, I'm going to run this medicine up to my mom and I'll be right back." Suddenly, his brain registered her bewildered expression. "What is it?"

Yasmine shook it off. "Someone just called on your phone. Hurry up. The movie is getting good."

"You stopped it, didn't you?"

"Uh, yeah."

Isaiah didn't believe her. "Rewind it back to where I left and I'll be back." He turned. "By the way, who called?" he asked, bounding up the stairs.

"Don't know," she yelled back. "Some woman."

He missed a step and fell forward. His knee banged against the stairs and he did a half roll onto his butt and slid down.

Yasmine ran to the staircase. "Are you all right?"

At the top of the stairs, his mother appeared. "What is all that racket?"

"He fell," Yasmine said, her eyes remaining on Isaiah as she waited for an answer.

"I'm fine, I'm fine," he said, feeling more than a little embarrassed.

Georgia rushed to him. "Are you sure you're all right?"

"Yes, yes." He turned toward Yas. "*Who* did you say called?"

She shrugged, and then a light flickered in her eyes. She rushed to retrieve his cell phone.

As sharp as ever, Georgia caught on to their conversation and squeezed his shoulder. "Did your lady friend call?"

Yasmine reappeared and handed him the phone. He quickly reviewed the last number received. "I don't believe it," he said, blinking. When he looked at the two women, a geyser of hope erupted in his chest. "She called."

* * *

"Are you sure you dialed the right number?" Toni asked when Brooklyn sat the cordless down on the coffee table.

"I'm sure. Some woman picked up. Might have been his girlfriend." A tinge of jealousy pricked.

Toni's frown deepened. "You don't know that. Could have been his mother for all you know."

"And it could have been a girlfriend. Anything could change in a man's life in six months. Especially someone as good looking as Isaiah."

"Would a man with a girlfriend send you gifts and flowers—and practically beg for you to call him?"

Brooklyn dropped a hand to her hip while her gaze turned into a narrowed stare.

Toni shook her head at the ridiculous question. "Okay. Forget I said that."

With a slow smile, Brooklyn reclaimed her wineglass and eased back into the sofa. "I don't know why I listen to you anyway. I'm not ready to jump back into a relationship."

Toni rolled her eyes. "Cut me a break. It's one thing to lie to me, it's another thing entirely when you start believing those lies."

"What the hell is that supposed to mean?"

"Just what I said." She shrugged. "Since your divorce, we repeat this same vignette. It's time for another scene, or act, or perhaps a whole new play."

Angry, Brooklyn bolted to her feet, ignoring her sudden head rush. "I'm so sorry my Shakespearean tragedy of a life is boring you. You might have said something sooner, I could've spared you the trip over here." She grabbed the empty wine bottle from the table and proceeded to march toward the kitchen.

"That's not what I meant." Toni jumped up and fell in line behind her. "I just think it's time to either piss or get off the pot, so to speak."

"Eloquent," Brooklyn said, shaking her head. "Has anyone ever told you that you have a way with words?" She grabbed yet another bottle of wine from the refrigerator, fully acknowledging this was the most she'd drunk since college.

"I mean it, Brooke. It's time to stop feeling sorry for yourself and move on. Evan and Macy don't seem to be mourning the failure of his marriage. He's ready to take the bull by the horns and try again."

"You don't get it. I don't want to try again." She popped open the bottle, and then stormed back into the living room with it.

Again, Toni followed behind her. "I'm not buying it. I think you do want a relationship. You're just too stubborn to admit it."

Brooklyn shook her head, not sure whether her confusion stemmed from Toni's speech or from the alcohol.

"You've been ready since the moment you slept with Mr. Fine in New York. This little song and dance you've been performing since then is because you're trying to figure out a way to give yourself permission to love again."

Incredulous, Brooklyn faced her friend. "Where

on earth do you get this weak-minded psychology crap?"

"It was my minor in college."

"Well, you're lousy at it."

Toni smirked. "The more you lash out the more I think I'm right." Toni picked up the cordless phone lying on the table and stretched it out toward Brooklyn. "Call him again. This time leave a message."

As if on cue, the phone rang.

Brooklyn and Toni's startled gazes riveted toward it and then lifted back at one another.

"Who is it?" Brooklyn asked, her voice a thin whisper.

"How in the hell would I know?" Toni continued to thrust the phone toward Brooklyn as it continued to ring.

Stepping back as though it were lethal, Brooklyn shook her head. Her brain muddled helplessly in its intoxicated state. "Read the caller ID screen," she instructed.

"Oh, for Pete's sake." Toni glanced at the small screen on the hand unit and a full smile bloomed across her face. "Isaiah Washington."

Brooklyn's heart dropped and anchored somewhere below her knees. "I don't want to answer it. Let it go to the answering machine. I'm not here." The excuses poured out of her in rapid succession.

Toni's smile turned wicked and Brooklyn watched in horror as Toni answered the call.

"Hello." She frowned, believing the caller might have hung up. "Hello," she said again.

"There. He hung up," Brooklyn whispered, reaching to snatch the phone away.

"Hello," a male voice finally said.

Toni dodged Brooklyn's reaching fingers. "Is this Isaiah?" she asked.

"Yes, I was returning your call. You did call, didn't you?" he asked.

Toni placed a hand over the mouthpiece. "Damn, he sounds sexy." She then spoke back into the phone. "No, that would've been my girlfriend, Brooklyn. I'm Toni."

"Hello, Toni. May I speak with Brooklyn?"

"Sure, she's *right* here."

Brooklyn waved her hands and backed away from the phone. She had no idea what to say to this man, especially when she was more than a little tipsy.

Toni held the phone toward her. "He wants to talk with you."

Trapped, Brooklyn's hands fell to her sides as she looked helplessly at the phone.

"Come on. You know you want to talk to him."

The truth was difficult to accept. She reached for the phone and prayed she wouldn't make a fool of herself. "Hello, Isaiah."

"Good evening, Brooklyn." His low, seductive baritone flowed over her like a feathery caress. "I'm glad you called."

Brooklyn sat down, hoping the action would do

something about the crazy knots forming in her stomach. "I'm sorry it took so long."

Toni sat beside her and leaned over to hear what was being said.

Annoyed, Brooklyn swiveled away. "How are you?"

"Better now that you've called." He chuckled.

Regret and shame raged within Brooklyn while she struggled to clear her head. "I should have called sooner, but, um, I guess I was a bit embarrassed for the way I treated you the other night."

"And on the highway."

She placed a hand over her eyes. How could she have forgotten about that? "Yeah, I was awful to you then, too."

"And for disappearing on me in New York."

Reeling back against the sofa's plump pillows, Brooklyn allowed shame to win the battle. "All right, all right. I've pretty much treated you like crap. I'm sorry."

"Apology accepted."

"You know, now that you've pointed out how mean I've been toward you, why are you still interested?"

"I don't know. Maybe I'm hoping in the end you'll be worth the trouble."

"I can't promise you that."

His sexy laugh returned. "No, I don't think you can."

She laughed, too, and then realized she'd wanted to talk to him for the last six months. The night they'd met, he'd been so easy to talk to, laugh with . . . and even make love to.

"I want to see you again," he said.

Her breath hitched at the seriousness of his tone and she hesitated to give voice to her own desires.

"Brooklyn?" he asked. "Are you still there?"

Slowly, she released her breath. "I'm still here," she managed to say and cast a futile glance at Toni before admitting the truth. "I want to see you, too."

A fusion of hope, joy, and relief exploded within Isaiah. Had he been alone, he might have performed a touchdown dance throughout the living room. Instead, he refrained and sat composed with a face-splitting smile. "Then when can I see you?"

"I don't know." Her voice quivered. "How about sometime next week?"

"How about tomorrow?"

"Tomorrow?"

"Good," he said, realizing he shouldn't give her too much time to think it over. She might try to back out of it. "Eight o'clock?"

"Oh, I don't know." She paused. "Eight o'clock seems so—"

"Good point. We better make it seven. I've already taken the liberty of looking you up in the phone book—hope you don't mind. I'll pick you up tomorrow at seven," he said, trying to keep his hopefulness out of his voice. She could easily shoot him down at any time.

Unsure of when she'd lost control or the ability to keep up with the conversation, she simply resigned in defeat. "Tomorrow at seven. I'll be ready."

She disconnected the call and stared down at the phone.

Toni's arms swung around her friend as she burst with excitement. "Sounds like you're going to get laid again."

Fifteen

The next day flew by at warp speed. By the time Brooklyn made it home to prepare for her date, she was a basket case. She rifled through her closet and tried on every outfit—twice. The problem was she had no clue to where Isaiah planned to take her.

"Maybe I should call him," she whispered and eyed the phone next to the bed. The very idea heightened her anxiety. She waved off the notion, but reason demanded that she call.

Retrieving Isaiah's business card, she sat on the edge of the bed and stared at the phone. "Just do it—but stay casual, and keep it light," she coached herself, and then exhaled a long, tired breath and picked up the receiver.

Isaiah barely heard his cell above his singing and electric razor and hoped the call wasn't business related. He answered without reviewing the caller ID. "Hello."

"Hello. Isaiah?"

Dread clawed through him. "Brooklyn. Don't tell me you've called to cancel."

"Oh, no. It's nothing like that." She chuckled with a slight tremor. "I was just wondering where we were going tonight. I have no idea how to dress for our date."

Relieved, he laughed. "In that case, it's going to be a formal evening—so put on your best dress."

"Really? Any way I can get you to give me a hint to where you're taking me?"

Isaiah smiled and leaned against the bathroom's door frame. "Sorry, Charlie. It's going to be a surprise."

"Not even a little hint?" she purred.

"Sounding like that, you're making it hard to say no."

"Then don't."

He laughed. "Don't you like surprises?"

"Depends."

"Trust me. You'll like this surprise."

She sighed, but a smile lingered on her lips. "All right, you win. I'll see you at seven."

"On the dot," he joked, and then disconnected the call. When he turned and faced his reflection in the mirror, he winked. "You have a date with an angel."

As it turned out that evening, the worst storm Isaiah had experienced in years descended on Atlanta. Lightning littered the sky while claps of thunder rattled him as he searched for Brooklyn's address. The rental car's navigation system had gone haywire, and now he was lost and more than an hour late for his date.

When the house finally materialized, relief overwhelmed him. He parked in the driveway, grabbed the umbrella and the bundle of roses from the passenger seat, and then made a mad dash to the front porch.

A gust of wind yanked the umbrella from his hand before he had a chance to think. He turned and watched as it landed in the front yard. Cursing, he rushed after it. By the time he made it beneath the relative shelter of the front porch, he was a mess.

He rang the doorbell.

The door opened and a gorgeous Brooklyn Douglas stared back at him.

"Oh, my goodness." Her gaze traveled over him with open shock and concern. "Are you all right?"

Isaiah's annoyance at his ruined evening vanished at first sight of her. A stunning red dress hugged her Coke-bottle figure like a second layer of skin while the garment's deep neckline showcased her ample bosom. She wore her hair pinned up, which forced him to admire her elegant neck and jawline.

"Are you all right?" she asked again, waving a hand in front of him to break his trance.

Isaiah blinked and stared into her brown eyes. "You're beautiful," he whispered.

Her face flushed a deep burgundy. "I wish I

could say the same for you. Let's get you dry." She turned and gestured for him to follow.

Isaiah complied, cringing at the feel of his wet clothes plastered against him. Once inside, he remembered the roses. "For you."

"Oh." She closed the door and smiled. "Thank you, but you shouldn't have. You've already sent me enough flowers to open my own shop."

He laughed. "Maybe I did overdo it a bit."

Thunder boomed overhead and the lights flickered.

"Seems like we're in for a doozy." She cast a worried look in his direction.

"Yeah. I think it's safe to say we're not going to make our reservations."

Brooklyn's smile widened. "The first thing we need to do is get you out of those clothes."

His brows knitted. "Sounds like this date is starting to look up."

Laughing, she turned away. "Follow me and I'll see if I can find you something to put on."

Minutes later, Isaiah stripped down in Brooklyn's son's bedroom and donned a large, baby-blue robe she'd laid out.

While Isaiah cleaned up, Brooklyn rummaged through the refrigerator to find something quick and easy for dinner. As she did that, she couldn't stop snickering at the memory of a drenched Isaiah at her front door.

"Something funny?" Isaiah asked.

Startled, she blinked up at him. He filled out

her son's robe nicely, more so than Jaleel had ever come close to doing.

He lifted a curious brow when her eyes finally met his.

"You could say that," she said, choosing to remain ambiguous. She pulled out a Tupperware container from the refrigerator. "I hope you like meat loaf."

"Love it." He winked.

She turned and pulled down a few cans of vegetables. "I'm sorry this isn't a gourmet dinner, but it's the best I can do on such short notice."

"Tell you what. Since I'm supposed to be treating you, why don't you sit down and let me take over?" He cupped an arm under her elbow and guided her to the other side of the breakfast bar.

"You cook?" she asked, unable to hide her surprise.

"I dabble a little."

"Uh-huh." She eased onto a stool. "Just try not to burn down my kitchen."

His lips curled with a laugh. "I think I can manage that. How about I fix us something a little special?"

"I'm game."

"Great. Let's see what else is in the refrigerator."

Other than dispensing a few directions as to where the skillets and ingredients were stored, Brooklyn watched with unadulterated pleasure as Isaiah prepared their meal. As she observed him, it became clear he did more than just dabble.

In fact, the longer she watched, the more relieved she was for not serving her mediocre meat loaf.

"So where did you learn to cook?"

"Actually, it's just something I picked up over the years. Plus, it's a great way to impress women." He cast her a sidelong glance. "Are you impressed?"

"Very."

"Good. I aim to please."

Her brows quirked. "I'll keep that in mind."

He chuckled under his breath, and then returned his attention to the task at hand.

Thirty minutes later, while sitting across from each other in the dining room brightened with candles, Brooklyn sank her teeth into the most delicious chicken primavera she'd ever tasted. Her eyes drifted closed as she emitted a soft moan. "I'm in love."

"Well, I don't know what to say," Isaiah joked. "It's so soon."

She opened her eyes. "I meant with the food," she said with playful sarcasm.

His lips twitched. "Sure you did."

Brooklyn flushed. The sight of him in such an intimate setting and dressed in so little seemed like the most natural thing in the world.

In the distance, thunder rolled and the rain's rhythm quickened against the windows.

"Sounds like the storm is picking up again," Isaiah commented. "I guess I should view the Weather Channel before planning our next date."

Her brows rose inquisitively.

His smile sloped as awkward bemusement transformed his features. "That's *if* you agree to see me again."

"There may be a strong possibility of that," she said with no hint of the wave of uncertainty crashing within her. His pewter gaze twinkled, which did nothing to pacify her raging hormones. She took another bite of her food and her eyes drifted to half-moons as another moan escaped her lips.

When he chuckled, her eyes snapped open. "Sorry."

He held up his hand. "Please, don't apologize. I can listen to you all night."

The sexual reference wasn't lost on Brooklyn. "I just bet you could."

His laugh deepened. "In case I haven't told you, I'm glad our paths crossed again."

"I am, too," she said, and meant it.

Their gazes fused and, suddenly, neither heard the storm outside. However, the temperature inside jumped. They smiled and allowed their gazes to drift apart.

"I'm curious about something," Brooklyn said after a lengthy silence.

"Oh?"

"What brought you to Atlanta?"

His lips flattened slightly. "My mother suffered a stoke."

She blinked in surprise. "I'm so sorry," she said. "How is she?"

"Remarkably better," he said, cocking his head. "She's a little slow getting around, but she's de-

termined to resume living her life as though nothing has happened—no matter how much I
protest."

His open affection toward his mother touched
Brooklyn. "I've always said you could tell a good
man by the way he treats his mother."

Amusement returned to his handsome features.
"Is that right?"

She bobbed her head. "Yep."

"So you think I'm a good man?"

As she smacked a hand against her forehead,
her body quaked with laughter. "I guess I walked
right into that one."

"Yes, ma'am. And mind you, I'm waiting for an
answer."

"You're all right." She shrugged.

"Just all right?" He rolled his eyes heavenward.
"Boy, you're a tough cookie."

She shrugged again. Maybe she was being hard
on him. After all, he was kind, considerate, an excellent cook . . . and a great lover. Her gaze lowered
to the exposed patch of flesh beneath his robe.

Isaiah cleared his throat. "About the other
night—"

Brooklyn groaned and covered her eyes. She
wanted to forget about the night she'd barged
over to Evan's screaming like a banshee.

He laughed at her obvious embarrassment.

"I thought you'd accepted my apology about
that night," she said.

"I have. I'm curious about something else."

She frowned. "About what?"

It was his turn to shrug.

When he didn't immediately launch into his question, she noticed he looked uncomfortable. "What is it?"

Their gazes locked.

"Are you still in love with your ex-husband?"

Brooklyn rocked back with a burst of laughter. "Good heavens, no." That was the last question she'd expected.

Isaiah's relief reflected in a breathtaking smile.

"That's certainly good to hear," he remarked, but caution remained in his demeanor. "Do you think he's still in love with you?"

Suddenly, she was curious about what prompted this line of questioning. "I doubt it." She watched him as he nodded. "Why do you ask?" This time when he shrugged, she didn't believe his act of nonchalance.

"No reason."

"You," she said with a weak smile, "are a bad liar."

"So my best friend keeps telling me."

Her lips widened while she waited for a real answer.

"Your ex-husband's guess of our true relationship gave me the distinct impression that he was jealous."

"Our true relationship?" Brooklyn repeated, lowering her fork so she could bridge her hand beneath her chin. "What exactly *is* our true relationship?"

Isaiah cocked his head as he maintained eye

contact. "I think we fall into the category of lovers."

"One night—"

"So far."

Brooklyn's body jerked from the impact of his words and try as she might, she couldn't pull her gaze away from his intense stare.

His smile turned devilish and the room's temperature increased another ten degrees. "Of course, this is totally up to you."

"Are you telling me that you only asked me out for a repeat performance of our time in New York?"

"Isn't it the same reason why you accepted?"

Cornered by the question, Brooklyn slid on a brave face, though she couldn't help but feel a flicker of disappointment. "We did have a nice time."

"Just nice?" An infectious rumble of laughter filled the space between them.

"Okay, it was better than 'nice.'"

"I'd like to say it was *earth-shattering*." His brows jiggled playfully above his twinkling gray eyes.

She crossed her arms. *"Mind-blowing."*

In a blink, his amusement faded into seriousness. "It was *amazing*."

"Incredible."

Heat radiated between them, transforming the room into a sweltering sauna. Isaiah controlled his primal urge to pounce, but his desire to have her heaving passionately beneath him did propel him to his feet.

Brooklyn stood. Her gaze followed him as he

neared. Her entire body ached to be touched. When he stopped before her, she could only hear the blood rushing into her head.

He cradled her chin between his fingers. "I've missed you."

She leaned into his touch; the wondrous fusion of fire and ice sucked the air from her lungs. However, he didn't wait to hear her response. He leaned toward her. The precious few seconds it took for their lips to connect felt like an eternity.

The familiar taste of him was like a sweet homecoming to her feral emotions as her arms encircled and drew him closer.

Their kiss grew hungry, neither seemingly able to get enough of the other.

As his hands traveled down the length of her back, a quiver of pleasure followed in their wake. His hot mouth nuzzled the column of her neck and she couldn't stop the tremor in her knees.

She nipped at the lobe of his ear and smiled wickedly at his sharp intake of breath. He wanted her as much as she needed him. Why should they continue to pretend otherwise?

He unzipped her dress.

"I want you." His husky proclamation penetrated the thick cloud of desire that encircled her brain.

"I need you," she answered in honest, careless abandonment. She brought her hands down against his muscled chest and experienced another heat wave.

Isaiah bent forward and before she knew it,

he'd swept her up into his arms. "Where's the bedroom?"

If she was going to protest, this would be the time to do it, she realized. "Upstairs. First door on your right."

He rewarded her with another breathtaking smile, and then kissed her again with the same mindless passion before carrying her out of the dining room and up the stairs toward her bed.

A SPECIAL "THANK YOU" FROM ARABESQUE JUST FOR YOU!

Send this card back and you'll receive 4 FREE Arabesque Novels—a $25.96 value—absolutely FREE!

The introductory 4 Arabesque Romance books are yours FREE (plus $1.99 shipping & handling). If you wish to continue to receive 4 books every month, do nothing. Each month, we will send you 4 New Arabesque Romance Novels for your free examination. If you wish to keep them, pay just $16* (plus, $1.99 shipping & handling). If you decide not to continue, you owe nothing!

- Send no money now.
- Never an obligation.
- Books delivered to your door!

We hope that after receiving your FREE books you'll want to remain an Arabesque subscriber, but the choice is yours! So why not take advantage of this Arabesque offer, with no risk of any kind. You'll be glad you did!

In fact, we're so sure you will love your Arabesque novels, that we will send you an Arabesque Tote Bag FREE with your first paid shipment.

Call Us TOLL-FREE At 1-888-345-BOOK

* Prices subject to change

THE "THANK YOU" GIFT INCLUDES:

- 4 books absolutely FREE (plus $1.99 for shipping and handling).
- A FREE newsletter, *Arabesque Romance News*, filled with author interviews, book previews, special offers, and more!
- No risks or obligations.

INTRODUCTORY OFFER CERTIFICATE

Yes! Please send me 4 FREE Arabesque novels (plus $1.99 for shipping & handling). I am under no obligation to purchase any books, as explained on the back of this card. Send my **FREE Tote Bag** after my first regular paid shipment.

NAME _____

ADDRESS _____ APT. _____

CITY _____ STATE _____ ZIP _____

TELEPHONE ( ) _____

E-MAIL _____

SIGNATURE _____

Thank You!

AN073A

ARABESQUE

Accepting the four introductory books for FREE (plus $1.99 to offset the cost of shipping & handling) places you under no obligation to buy anything. You may keep the books and return the shipping statement marked "cancelled". If you do not cancel, about a month later we will send 4 additional Arabesque novels, and you will be billed the preferred subscriber's price of just $4.00 per title. That's $16.00* for all 4 books for a savings of almost 40% off the cover price (Plus $1.99 for shipping and handling). You may cancel at any time, but if you choose to continue, every month we'll send you 4 more books, which you may either purchase at the preferred discount price. . . or return to us and cancel your subscription.

* PRICES SUBJECT TO CHANGE

THE ARABESQUE ROMANCE BOOK CLUB
P.O. BOX 5214
CLIFTON NJ 07015-5214

PLACE
STAMP
HERE

Relax and
Enjoy the Ride

Sixteen

Isaiah lowered Brooklyn onto the bed. The sweet nectar of her kisses pushed him near the edge of madness. She tasted too good and felt so right lying beneath him. No other woman had ignited this fire—this longing within him.

He nuzzled her neck, the gentle slope of her shoulder, and then grew hard at the sound of his name tumbling from her lips. With a patience he didn't feel, he peeled the thin straps of her dress from her shoulders and pushed the gown down and off her luscious body.

He sucked in a breath at the sight of her red satin and lace lingerie.

She charmed him with a sly smile and while he was distracted, she tugged the belt of his robe, and then pushed the thick material off.

He hovered above her while her arms looped possessively around his shoulders. A strobe of lightning flashed outside the window and enabled him to read so much in her sparkling gaze.

His mouth covered hers and he was instantly

drunk with passion. He cupped her breasts and his arousal heightened at the feel of their fullness.

Brooklyn broke their kiss and drew in deep shaky breaths. "I need to ask you something."

Talk? She wants to talk? Lord, please say she doesn't want to talk. He, too, drew in a deep breath and spoke in a feigned patience. "Okay."

"Do you have a condom?"

Suddenly, Isaiah wondered if she would think less of him if he just started crying. He rolled off of her and dropped his head into his hands. "You're not going to believe this."

To his amazement, she laughed.

He shook his head. "I meant to stop by the pharmacy on my way—well, in case something like this happened. With the storm and everything I guess I forgot." He sighed and cast a sidelong glance at her.

Her laughter deepened.

Isaiah shook his head. "I fail to see what is so funny," he said in a near pout.

"We are," she announced. "I mean, even my son . . ."

He frowned. "What?" There was something erotic and conspiratorial about the latest curve of her lips.

"I'll be right back," she said, and then stood from the bed.

Isaiah groaned with lustful appreciation of her beautiful legs clad in thigh-high stockings. The red garter belt and high shoes were a nice touch, too. Slowly, it dawned on him that she was about to the leave the room. "Where are you going?"

Despite the low lighting, he witnessed a slight flush to her golden skin.

"I think I have the solution to our problem."

His brows rose in mild surprise and the hope that all was not lost galloped through his veins.

"Stay here," she said and slipped through the door.

Was she kidding? Wild horses couldn't drag him away. He smiled, leaned back, and crossed his arms behind his head. "I'll be right here."

Brooklyn couldn't believe what she was about to do as she walked into her son's bedroom. Guilt told her she should be ashamed of herself while the other half of her conscience encouraged her to hurry.

She crossed over to Jaleel's chest of drawers and rummaged through its contents. A whiplash of disappointment hit her when her initial search came up empty. Her hands became a frenzy of movement and she literally jumped when she hit two boxes buried toward the back.

Relief and disbelief assailed her. "I'm going to need counseling after this," she admitted under her breath. "Orgasm control?" She shook her head and opened the new box. "Popular brand." She withdrew two condoms, and then stopped before putting the package back. She and Isaiah had definitely used more than two the last time they were together.

"I'll just take a box and replace it later," she decided and shoved her son's clothes back into the drawer, and then rushed back to her bedroom.

Isaiah sat up. "There you are. I was starting to worry."

She held up the box of condoms. "Jackpot." His deep rumble of laughter warmed her and she smiled back at him in the semidarkness. She turned and moved toward her dresser and found the lighter she kept in a glass bowl.

"I think we need some more light." She walked around the room and lit the lavender-scented candles that were strategically placed throughout the room. "There. That's better." She turned and faced him.

Isaiah stood from the bed. The beauty of his naked form immediately thinned Brooklyn's breath as he strolled toward her.

He smiled when he stopped in front of her. "Do you still want to go through with this?" He slid a hand along the side of her face.

She smiled. "You still talk too much. I'm just sorry I missed your undressing."

His soft chuckle was like a mild aphrodisiac. At his head's slow descent, her knees weakened at the feel of his warm breath against her skin. When his lips pressed against hers, all thoughts vanished.

Suddenly, his hands and mouth were everywhere and still it wasn't enough. Soon, she couldn't tell his ragged breathing apart from her own.

Again, he swept her into his arms, carried her back to the bed, and burned a trail of kisses down the column of her neck. Then, he removed her bra with the skill of a magician.

His lips claimed an aroused nipple and Brooklyn writhed beneath him, convinced she would drown in an ocean of euphoria.

Mindlessly, her hands roamed across the span of his back, while a small flame ignited within her.

"I love the way you taste," he moaned.

The erotic praise emboldened her to do her own tasting. She kissed his shoulders, his chest, and then flicked her tongue across his hard nipples.

He sucked in a breath. "Good Lord. You're going to be my undoing."

"Promise?" She joined him in his amusement as she slowly rolled onto her side, and then over to claim the top position.

Their familiar dance for dominance became a titillating performance they both enjoyed.

While she continued to pay homage to his muscled chest, she was more than aware of his hands unsnapping the hooks of her garter belt and relieving her of her panties.

She relinquished the top position without protest and when his magic fingers dipped between her silky walls, she could only manage a gasp of pleasure.

Isaiah's tongue invaded her mouth. In no time at all his fingers and mouth collaborated to work in the same mind-shattering rhythm.

After a long while, Brooklyn tore her lips away to cry out her body's orgasmic explosion—and still his hands didn't stop. She inched up the bed while she locked her hands against his arm in a vain attempt to stop his sweet assault.

She tried to beg him to stop, but failed. Another orgasm gripped her, but her cries were muffled by Isaiah's mouth.

He reached down on the bed and retrieved the box of condoms.

"Why don't you help me?" he asked huskily.

"With pleasure," she responded in a tone that rivaled his own. Tenderly, her hands teased against his hard shaft before she actually slid on the condom.

When she'd finished, he grabbed her hands and locked them above her head.

"Oh, you're going to pay for that," he warned.

"Promise?"

His response was the gentle entrance into her body.

Brooklyn sucked in as much air as her lungs would allow as the sheer size of him filled her completely.

He kept her hands pinned above her while their hips began a slow rock.

She locked her legs around him and met his movements—thrust for thrust in a competition they both intended to win.

Music played in her head. It was the same orchestra from that long ago wintry morning. This was paradise—she was sure of it.

For Isaiah, he was positive he'd returned to heaven. The simple smell, taste, and feel of her were like no other homecoming he'd known.

After long minutes of slow, deliberate moves, his passion took over and his tempo quickened. He plunged deeper and reveled in the sound of her moans as they grew louder.

Tears slid from the corners of her eyes. She was overwhelmed by his sweet torment. Her head thrashed in wanton abandonment against the pillows and soon a familiar fire lit within her intimate core, and then blazed into an inferno.

Isaiah sucked in a breath through clenched teeth; his thrusts had transformed into a frenzy of jerky movements as he neared the finish line.

Together, their bodies shook with a violent eruption as his roar and her cry of release blended into a unique crescendo.

He fell limp against her, and then carefully rolled to her side. For a long moment, neither spoke. Well aware of the other's stamina, they both knew that this was merely an intermission before the next act. Taking advantage of the calm, Isaiah pulled Brooklyn against him. This woman had captivated his heart and mind like no other. And he vowed that this time, he would never let her go.

Seventeen

Brooklyn awoke cocooned in a mesh of arms and legs, and this time gave thanks for last night not being a dream. She smiled and stretched against Isaiah, but stifled her movements when she brushed against his arousal.

"You're finally awake," Isaiah said from behind her.

Her smile widened as she wiggled her rump against him. "I can tell you are, too."

He kissed the back of her head. "Don't start anything you can't finish," he warned with mild amusement.

She wiggled again and laughed out loud when he threw the covers back and flipped her over to face him.

They were both naked, compliments of their early morning shower. Their skins were soft, too, thanks to an even later baby oil contest.

"I thought by now you would've had enough," Isaiah said, capturing a kiss.

Brooklyn melted and greedily accepted all he had to offer. When his lips withdrew, she gave him a timid smile. "I don't think I can ever get enough of you."

His gray eyes twinkled as he smiled. "I can't tell you how good that is to hear." This time when his head descended, his mouth settled on an erect nipple.

Lazily, she closed her eyes and enjoyed his tongue's playful teasing. In no time, her body came alive beneath his skillful sorcery. After a while, his mouth finished its quiet worship with her breasts and traveled lower along the length of her body, settling at the soft triangle of curls between her legs.

Brooklyn bit her lower lip and ran her fingers through his hair. Then, her breath hitched and a jumble of words spilled from her lips.

He slid his hands beneath her to give him better access and control.

Her orgasm slammed into her with the force of a locomotive and she tried her best to wiggle away from Isaiah's ravishing mouth. When it was clear that she couldn't, she was reduced to begging for mercy.

Isaiah released her. He laughed as he crawled up the bed beside her and slid on a new condom. "Don't say I didn't warn you."

For his remark, she gave him a hard smack against the shoulder. "You don't play fair." She swiped a pillow at his head.

He ducked beneath another pillow and proclaimed, "All is fair in love and war."

"Is that right?" She climbed on top of him and

tried to wrestle the pillow away from his face. When that didn't work, she tickled his sides.

He relinquished his hold and tried to grab hold of her arms.

Brooklyn locked her legs at his sides while he bucked beneath her. Hit with a flash of inspiration, she stopped—just long enough to reposition herself.

Isaiah removed the pillow from his face and was about to say something when Brooklyn attacked his sides again. At the first thrust of his hips, he slid easily into her. His eyes rounded in pleasant surprise.

"All is fair in love and war," she reminded him with a wicked smile and then leaned forward to steal a kiss.

"You're a quick learner," he praised when their lips separated.

"Well, let me show you what else I've learned," she said, grabbing his arms and pinning them above his head. "Remember this?" In a painfully slow rhythm, she rocked her hips, and then flashed him a victorious smile when a low groan rumbled from his chest.

"Damn, you *are* good," he said. He watched her through the haze of his lashes, while his thoughts turned to mush from the exquisite feel of her.

Brooklyn took her time and relished the way he completely filled her. After a time, her gentle rocking quickened and she released his hands to submit to the glorious feeling building inside her.

Isaiah's hands settled against her hips as he now joined in and pumped in the same madding pace.

Their breathing came hard and fast. Each clung to the other as though their very lives depended on their reaching this marvelous pinnacle together.

Brooklyn's cry of ecstasy overpowered his rough shout for the Almighty. And when she collapsed against him, they laughed at what had just transpired.

"You're trying to kill me," he panted.

"What gave me away?"

He laughed and kissed the top of her head. "So," Isaiah said and leaned up to place a kiss against her forehead, "what does a man have to do to get some nourishment around here?"

She nuzzled closer. "Ah, the man wants breakfast."

"I can't possibly be the only one. We both had quite a workout."

At that moment, a loud and long growl resonated from Brooklyn's stomach and she winced with embarrassment.

"I guess that answers my question," he said, kissing her again.

With a skill and grace that amazed her, Isaiah sat up and then stood from the bed with her body still clasped around him. She giggled and held on tight as he carried her to the adjoining bathroom.

In the shower, Isaiah took his time washing her incredible body, not to mention the hard time he had remembering the object was to clean her and not muss her up again. And he would have been successful, too, had she not shattered his determination by teasing him mercilessly when it was her turn to wash him. In no time at all, he had her wet body pressed up against the tile.

By the time they made it to the kitchen, it was really time for lunch. They started off with the greatest of intentions: to fix a couple of sandwiches. But after two bites, the kitchen counter was wiped clean and Brooklyn was laid out for a different kind of feast.

Soon, only a few rooms were saved from their all-day sex-a-thon. The rain had returned with the setting sun, and the reacquainted lovers lay spent in front of the fireplace in the living room.

Once rested, they talked and shared intimate details about their lives.

"I don't believe it," she said. "She actually left you for your uncle?" She was propped up at his side.

He shrugged. "Who can understand love?"

She studied him as if trying to discern whether his expression would belie his words. Then, she shrugged as well. "Yeah. I guess you're right."

He smiled and reached out to push a lock of hair behind her ears. "Simply beautiful."

She flushed and drew the number eight on his chest with her finger. "You know, while you were telling me about Cadence, I don't remember you ever mentioning the word love." She met his gaze. "Did you love her?"

He frowned while he contemplated the question. "I loved her, but I was never *in* love with her." He shrugged again. "I never understood why that was. Cadence is a lovely woman and she deserved more than I could give. I don't fault her for leaving."

"But with your uncle?" Brooklyn shook her head as she studied him. "Doesn't it feel like some type of betrayal for her to choose him? I mean, of all the men she could have chosen—why him?"

"Yes and no." He shifted to lay on his side and Brooklyn lay down so that she looked up at him. "Look, I'm not going to lie to you and tell you that it's easy whenever I see them together. But I understand why it happened. Maybe one day we all can be in the same room and there'll be no animosity."

Brooklyn released a long sigh while her thoughts traveled to her own situation. "I have to bow my head to you because you're a better person than I. I don't think I can ever forgive Evan and Macy."

He leaned down and kissed her. When he withdrew, his gaze bore into her. "I know it may seem as though you can't, but there will come a day when you'll have to let go of your anger. Either that or it'll rot and fester inside of you."

"Experience?"

He nodded. "Take my word. Figure out a way to forgive and move on."

She considered his words and snuggled closer.

Isaiah eased one arm beneath her head, and then draped the other over the curve of her hip. "Let's talk about happier things—like us." His comment successfully won a soft laugh from her, which in turn won a small smile from him.

"What about us?" She looked up at him. "Aren't you having a good time?"

He laughed and rolled her onto her back; his growing erection was a mere wisp away from her dewy entry. "What do you think?"

"I think you're insatiable."

"Only when it comes to you." His lips pressed lightly against hers. When her mouth parted and her warm tongue invaded his mouth, the kiss turned hungry.

Brooklyn couldn't believe she was ready for another round. She also couldn't believe Isaiah had no trouble meeting and satisfying her every need. In fact, that was exactly what he did for the rest of the evening . . . and into the night.

Eighteen

Isaiah returned to his mother's home bright and early on Monday morning—and was totally surprised to see Yasmine's radiant face greet him at the door.

"It lives," she exclaimed as she bounced with excitement. Then, her gaze took in his rumpled suit. "What on earth happened to you?"

"Only the best thing that could ever happen," he said, and whistled as he passed her.

Her squeal of delight followed him up the stairs as she followed him to his bedroom. "Spill it, spill it, spill it. I want to hear everything," she demanded.

Isaiah shook his head, but couldn't stop smiling. "You know I never kiss and tell."

"You are today." She glanced at her watch. "You just came home after a thirty-six-hour date. If you think you're going to hold out on the details then you're sadly mistaken."

At the soft knock at the bedroom door, Yasmine and Isaiah turned to see a smiling Georgia.

"Good morning, Mom."

Georgia's eyes twinkled. "Is it?" She entered the room, pressing most of her weight down on her cane. "I take it you had a nice time on your date."

Isaiah flushed and averted his gaze. "I guess you could say that."

"My, my. Dating has certainly changed since my day." Her eyes twinkled. "I'm going downstairs and fix you a nice breakfast. You hurry down."

"That's not necessary, Mom. I'll do it."

"You'll do no such thing. I'm quite capable. Thank you."

When his mother vanished from the doorway, Yasmine looked to him and crossed her arms. "I want details. Heck, I might want to take a few notes."

Isaiah rolled his eyes. "I need to change. Don't you two have something else you need to do?"

"No."

"Well, I do." He laughed, and then tried to direct her toward the door.

She wouldn't budge.

"I don't believe this." He started unbuttoning his shirt as he headed to the adjoining bathroom.

However, in an impressive move, Yasmine cut him off. "You're not leaving this room until you tell me something—anything. Don't forget, I played I Spy for you."

"And I'm eternally grateful. Now, get out." This time he placed a hand under her elbow and dragged her toward the door.

"Okay, okay. I'll go if you answer one question for me."

He released her and folded his arms. "It depends on the question."

"All right." She, too, folded her arms while her features struggled to appear serious. "Was your date worse, equal to, or better than your time in New York?"

His lips twitched into an easy smile. "It was definitely better."

Brooklyn was having the best Monday she'd had in years. Not only did she wake up in a great mood, she also had three houses placed under contract before noon.

"I'm mad at you," Toni announced when they finally settled in their booth at Mick's for lunch.

Brooklyn looked up, startled. "Me? What did I do?"

"I called you like a hundred times yesterday. What did you do—take your phone off the hook?"

A wave of embarrassment washed over Brooklyn. "Oh, that."

"Yeah, that," Toni huffed. "You came crawling to me for help. I loan you my best dress and then nothing."

"Well, I did plan to call you as soon as the date ended, but there wasn't time."

"What do you mean there wasn't any time?"

"Well, actually—"

"Can I get you ladies something to drink?" a bright-eyed waiter asked, appearing from out of nowhere.

Brooklyn's shoulders sagged with relief. "Yes—"

"Could you please give us a few more minutes?" Toni flashed a look of warning in Brooklyn's direction.

The waiter frowned, and then recovered. "Of course, ma'am."

Brooklyn waited until he was out of earshot. "Don't you think you were a little rude?"

"I'll leave a big tip. Now, spill it. Why didn't you call me at the end of your date?" Toni perked at her friend's broad smile.

"I didn't call because . . ." Brooklyn looked around and then leaned forward to whisper, "because when Isaiah left my house, it was time for me to go to work this morning."

Toni's jaw dropped. "You've got to be kidding me."

Smug, Brooklyn leaned back against the booth. "Nope."

"Wow. That dress must have worked wonders."

Unable to stop herself from bragging, she met Toni's gaze. "It did—for the short time that I had it on."

Toni squealed, and then clamped a hand over her mouth when she remembered where she was.

Brooklyn glanced around. "Keep it down," she hissed when her heartbeat returned to normal.

Toni retrieved her cell phone.

"What are you doing?"

"I'm calling the girls. They're never going to believe this."

Brooklyn reached over and snatched the phone

away from her. "You will do no such thing. What I tell you doesn't leave this table. Is that clear?"

"You've got to be kidding me, right? Maria, Ashley, and Noel are waiting on pins and needles to find out how your date went."

"You told them?"

"Damn right. This date falls under current events and late-breaking news. Hell, now it sounds like it should go under sports as well."

Despite herself, Brooklyn laughed.

"I have to call them. It's under the Girlfriend Rule Book section one. All Juicy Sexual Encounters Must Be Reported. Check your handbook."

"You didn't tell me about what's-his-name the other night. I had to drag that out of you."

Toni rolled her eyes. "The key word is *juicy*. Pay attention."

"Whatever. I'll decide who I want to know what and when."

For a while Toni leaned back and stared at her. "How long am I supposed to be quiet about this?"

Brooklyn shrugged. "I don't know. A couple of weeks—months. I'll play it by ear."

Toni's features remained a mask of disbelief. "I'll never be able to figure you out. If I were you I'd scream at the top of my lungs—I got laid, I got laid."

Embarrassment blazed up Brooklyn's face. "Will you behave yourself?"

"I certainly will not. I'm ecstatic for you. You should be, too." A twinkle appeared in Toni's eyes and she inched closer to the edge of her seat. "Was he as good as you remember?"

"Better," Brooklyn said, already forgetting to weigh just how much she wanted to tell her friend.

"And you stayed in bed for two days?"

She giggled like a schoolgirl. "I wouldn't say that we only stayed in the bed."

Toni bounced in her seat and clamped a hand over her mouth to prevent her squeal from filling the restaurant.

Brooklyn shook her head and despite the smile on her face, her thoughts turned troubled.

"What is it?"

She shrugged and tried to play it off. "Nothing. I'm fine. I'm happy."

Toni's eyes narrowed. "Uh-huh. Then how come you don't look too happy?"

"I am," she insisted with a bright smile. "It's just . . ."

"What?"

Her smile dimmed as she studied her friend. "I'm just worried about where this is going. A part of me is expecting the bottom to drop out at any moment, you know? Like this man is too good to be true and I'm afraid that I'm going to get caught up in the moment."

"Its just sex, right?" Toni shrugged. "You made it clear that you weren't looking for a relationship, didn't you?"

Brooklyn folded her arms and leaned onto the table. "Well, we didn't really discuss it, but I told him before that a relationship wasn't possible."

"Then don't worry about it. Just relax and enjoy the ride."

* * *

"Are you sure this woman isn't a 'ho'?" Yasmine asked, leaning back on Isaiah's bed when he stepped out of the bathroom.

"What? What are you doing back in here?"

"I left and now I came back." Yasmine shrugged. "I think it's a good question."

"No, it's not." Isaiah failed to keep the irritation out of his voice. "By the way, what time is your flight today?"

"Why? Are you tired of me already?" Yasmine placed a hand over her heart and slid on a wounded expression.

"No, never, of course not—when do you leave?"

"Fine. Tonight, if you must know."

Isaiah put on his jeans beneath his robe, and then removed his robe altogether.

Georgia gasped as she entered her son's room. "There are ladies in the room."

He frowned. "You're my mother."

Her color deepened considerably. "I know, but I was referring to Yasmine."

Isaiah and Yasmine laughed.

"Trust me, Mom. The lady is not interested."

"Yeah and besides, I've seen him in a lot less." At the realization of what she'd said, her eyes rounded as she slapped a hand across her mouth.

Isaiah shook his head.

"I don't think I want to hear any more." Georgia frowned with disapproval.

Downstairs at breakfast, it was Georgia's turn

to interrogate Isaiah about his date. He went down the checklist of saying how wonderful and warm he believed Brooklyn to be. And yes, he was sure that Georgia would like her. He told her everything she needed to know, which *didn't* include details. When he was finished, he looked at his mother and found that she was studying him.

"What?"

She shrugged and took another sip of her coffee. "I guess I was hoping th**at** this woman would mean more to you than just a new bed partner."

His heart squeezed and he knew better than to be surprised that his mother could see straight through him. "She does."

She met his gaze again. "How can you tell? Life exists outside the bedroom. Love isn't something that's just found between the sheets." She smiled and patted his hand. "Anyone want some more coffee?" She stood from the table.

"Sure, I'd like some," Yasmine said with a flickering smile.

Isaiah shook his head.

When his mother left the table, Yasmine leaned over to him and whispered, "She's right. If Brooklyn does mean more to you than just a wham-bam-thank-you-ma'am, then you've sort of put the cart before the horse."

Isaiah nodded. "Maybe."

"What do you mean?"

"Brooklyn isn't looking for a horse. The last one sort of trampled over her, if you know what I mean."

They fell silent for a long moment before Yas-

mine asked, "Are you looking for a horse—
metaphorically speaking?"

"I wasn't before I met her."

"But now?"

"More than anything."

Later that evening, Isaiah appeared at Brooklyn's door with flowers and the intention of taking
her *out* for dinner. However, she had other plans
and a few hours later, the lovers lay spent in each
other's arms.

"What are you thinking about?" Brooklyn asked
as she rolled onto her side and stared down at
him.

Isaiah debated telling the truth. "I was thinking about us." He waited through the ensuing
silence.

"What about us?"

He reached up and slid his hand softly along the
side of her face. "Don't tell me that you've never
thought about us." When she didn't answer, he experienced a rush of panic. Did she still believe there
was no chance of a relationship for them?

"I assumed what we have was enough for you,"
she said in a thick voice.

He had a hard time deciphering whether she
was angry, but he decided to forge ahead. "I never
agreed to that."

Expelling a long sigh, Brooklyn flopped back
among the pillows.

Tension quickly filled the space between them,

to the point where he half expected her to kick him out of the house. But when the seconds ticked into minutes, he became concerned.

"Brooklyn?"

"I don't know if I'm ready to have this conversation," she answered in a tone he'd never heard from her.

This time he rolled over to gaze at her. She was more beautiful than ever with her hair splayed across the pillow and her lips swollen from their kisses. "I like you a lot, Brooklyn. I just want the opportunity to get to know you better *outside* of the bedroom. Surely, that isn't too much to ask."

The corners of her mouth curved slightly. "No. It's not too much to ask."

This time he recognized what he heard in her voice because it also reflected in her eyes: fear. He reached up and traced the lining of her chin. "We've both been hurt before."

She swallowed but her gaze never wavered from his. "It's a big step for me."

"For me, too. But let's just take this a day at a time, one date at a time."

Her smile broadened as she snuggled closer. "I think I can handle that."

Nineteen

Three weeks later

To celebrate the Fourth of July, Isaiah and Brooklyn planned a large picnic at Callaway Gardens with family and friends. Brooklyn contacted Jaleel despite believing the introductions would be awkward. However, Jaleel declined her offer.

"Don't worry about it," Toni reassured her as she plopped down on the edge of Brooklyn's bed. "I'm sure Evan is just showing him a good time."

"Maybe too good." Brooklyn massaged her temples. "Do you know Jaleel has only called me twice this summer? *Twice.*" She held her fingers up for emphasis.

"Don't let it get to you. He's enjoying his summer and so are you."

Brooklyn drew in a deep breath and exhaled in a long steady stream. "Now, let's hope Isaiah's mom likes me."

"Will you calm down?" Toni said, rolling her eyes. "His mother will love you." She shook her head when Brooklyn held up yet another sundress. "Orange is not your color."

"But what if she doesn't? The way Isaiah dotes on her, it's essential that she *more* than just likes me. I need her to *love* me."

Toni chuckled at her frantic ramblings. "What's this? Three weeks of dating and you're dying to impress the mother? Have you guys taken a turn toward the serious side?"

Brooklyn ignored the question. She'd spent the last few weeks refusing to analyze her growing affection toward Isaiah.

"Fine. Don't answer my question." Toni jumped up from the bed and crossed over to the walk-in closet. "I know what's happening despite your protests and denials. I am a lawyer, after all. I know what's going on—no matter how much B.S. you shovel my way."

Brooklyn's lips curled. "Think all you want. I just want his mom to like me."

"Whatever."

"Speaking of shoveling it, I thought you didn't like this Brian guy. So why is he going with us to Callaway?"

"I never said I didn't like him. I just said he was lousy in bed—but he's getting better."

Brooklyn gaped, and then smacked her girlfriend a high five. "You go, girl."

Isaiah held his cell phone tucked beneath his ear while he continued to load the rented SUV with enough food to feed a small army. On the other end, Yasmine droned on about how she and her girlfriend, Mary, would miss him during the holiday.

"So when are you coming back?" Yasmine asked. "Rotech isn't the same without you."

"Probably toward the end of the summer. Mom and I are having a great time."

"Come on. Who are you trying to fool? Your mother is fine. You're still there because of your new ladylove."

He laughed. "I plead the Fifth."

"I just bet you do." She joined in with a light chuckle. "So is she the one?"

Isaiah considered the question and decided not to play coy. "I think so."

"Then I'm happy for you, buddy. And I'd like to add that I think it's about time. Now I can stop worrying so much about you."

"Since when did you start?"

"It feels like a lifetime ago."

He could actually picture her smiling on the other end. "Thanks, Yas. It's good to know you're always in my corner."

"All right. Let's cut the mushy stuff. Are you planning to stay in Atlanta permanently or are you going to try and convince her to pack up and move to Texas?"

"I think I'm a ways off on posing either question." He pinched the bridge of his nose.

"Is she still afraid of commitment?"

"She's afraid of the *word.*"

"Wow. Her ex really did a number on her, huh?"

"Something like that," he said, shaking his head. "But I'm determined to break down her wall of resistance. Even if I have to do it one brick at a time."

Brooklyn found Brian Olson to be both handsome and humorous when she met him. She also saw how Toni lit up the moment he'd entered the house.

Brian guided Toni into his arms, kissed her, and then extended a wrapped bowl of some kind.

"What's this?" Toni asked.

"I know you told me not to bring anything, but I didn't feel right about that so I made some of my world-famous potato salad." He smiled. "I hope everybody likes it."

"I'm sure we will." Toni leaned up on her toes and gave him a quick peck on the cheek.

Brooklyn lifted a curious brow at the loving couple and fought all that was holy not to say, "Aha!"

"Brian, can I get you something to drink while we wait for Isaiah to arrive?"

"Sure. I'll take a beer, if you got one."

She took the bowl from Toni. "One beer coming up." She walked into the kitchen and, on cue, Toni followed.

"So, what do you think?" Toni asked, her eyes shining.

"About what?" Brooklyn smiled and purposely kept her back to Toni.

"About Brian. What do you think of him?"

Brooklyn opened the refrigerator and buried her head behind the door. "Oh, he's cute, I guess."

In a flash, Toni was at the refrigerator, glaring down at her. "Cute? That's all you can say—he's cute?"

"And thoughtful," Brooklyn said, withdrawing a Heineken and closing the door. "It was nice of him to bring the potato salad."

Toni worked her mouth, but no words came.

Brooklyn couldn't contain her amusement any longer and laughed as she hugged her friend. "He's handsome and I think he's taken with you."

The doorbell rang.

"I'll get it," Brian yelled out from the den.

Brooklyn's smile widened. "He's also extremely helpful."

Toni's interrogation would not be deterred. "How can you tell he's taken with me?"

Brooklyn shrugged. "Something about the way he looks at you."

"Really?"

"Really." Brooklyn moved over to a drawer and pulled out a bottle opener. "You know, I should be mad at you. All that crap you gave me about not being in love. You're crazy about that man. It was written all over you when he came in."

Heavy footsteps drew Brooklyn's attention to Isaiah's familiar figure coming toward them. A warm glow radiated from within as he flashed them a smile.

"Afternoon, ladies. Are we ready for our picnic?"

Brooklyn started to respond when Toni dabbed something from her cheek. "What is it? Do I have something on my face?"

Toni smiled. "No. It just looked like you had something written on it."

By the time the small group arrived at Callaway Gardens, Brooklyn's spirits were at an all-time high. Brian turned out to be quite the comedian and had everyone bursting at the seams during the hourlong drive. Once there, and despite the already large crowd, they picked out a great spot near the lake where the fireworks would take place.

"Yo, man. This is a ridiculous amount of food you got here." Brian marveled at the spread before him.

Isaiah's face split into a wide grin. "Yeah, I guess you can say we sort of got carried away."

"Hmmph," Georgia cut in. "We nothing. Isaiah wouldn't let me so much as boil an egg. He was too busy trying to impress a certain girl," she added with twinkling eyes.

"Oooh." Toni and Brian turned knowing eyes toward Brooklyn.

Under such scrutiny, she couldn't help but blush.

Georgia reached over and squeezed her hand. "Frankly, I don't think he could've chosen a more lovely woman."

Brooklyn's embarrassment deepened. "Thank you."

Soon, the paper plates and plastic cups were passed and everyone dug in.

Afterward, when everyone was miserable from eating too much, Toni leaned back in Brian's arms and said to Isaiah, "Hell, if Brooklyn doesn't marry you, I will."

"Hey," Brian protested with sad puppy-dog eyes. "I was going to say the same thing."

Everyone cracked up.

"Sorry, bro. I don't swing that way," Isaiah said, easing closer toward Brooklyn. "This is all I can handle. Ain't that right, baby?" He leaned down for a kiss.

"That's right, honey."

Brian looked to Toni. "I guess it's our loss."

"So it would seem."

Georgia shook her head with mild amusement.

Upon meeting Georgia, Brooklyn understood where Isaiah had inherited his kind nature. The resemblance between mother and son was striking.

"I think I want to go for a walk," Toni announced, and then looked to Brian. "You want to join me?"

"You bet. I need to walk off some of this food."

They cleaned their area and stood to leave.

"We'll check back in with you guys later," Toni said, looping her arm through her boyfriend's as they strolled off.

"Now, don't they make a nice couple?" Georgia said, watching them.

Brooklyn nodded with a wide smile. "Yes, they do."

"Well, there you guys are." A male voice drifted toward them.

Isaiah looked up and was astonished to see Dr. Ramsey approaching them.

Georgia clapped her hands together. "Paul, I'm so glad you made it."

Dr. Ramsey's face split into a wide grin as he knelt beside her. "I've been looking everywhere. I've forgotten just how big this place is."

Isaiah couldn't stop staring.

Brooklyn leaned around him and offered her hand when the doctor sat next to Georgia.

"Hello. I'm Brooklyn."

"Paul Ramsey. A pleasure to meet you." He turned his gaze toward Isaiah. "It's good to see you again."

"Same here," Isaiah said without conviction.

His mother laughed. "I think he's in shock." She leaned over and patted her son's leg. "Don't have a conniption. Paul and I are just good friends."

"And dance partners," Paul added with a boastful grin. "Came in second place at the Senior Ball tournament."

Brooklyn perked up. "You two are ballroom dancers? How exciting. I've always wanted to do something like that. Unfortunately, I have two left feet, but a girl can always dream."

Georgia's face lit up as her words flowed with a rush of excitement. "I used to think the same way. Lord knows I could never drag Melvin to something like that." She leaned over toward Paul. "But I found a willing victim in Paul here."

"Oh, how nice." Brooklyn looked to Isaiah. "Don't you think that's nice?"

Not particularly. "Yeah, it's real nice." He flashed a quick smile, and then grew serious. "And just how long have you two been dance partners?"

"Oh, I don't know." His mother shrugged and looked to Paul. "It's been about three or four years. Wouldn't you say?"

"Five years, next Sunday," Paul corrected with a firm nod of his head.

Georgia brightened with astonishment. "You don't say? Has it been that long?"

"Yeah. You don't say," Isaiah said in a tone opposite of his mother's. Inwardly, his emotions dueled. On one hand, he should be happy his mother had found companionship, but on the other hand, he couldn't explain his apprehension.

"Sooo." Isaiah struggled to sound casual. "How come you didn't tell me about your dancing ambitions, lessons, and *partner?*" To his left, he heard snickering, but he ignored it and continued to stare at his mother.

His mother's eyes twinkled as she met his gaze. "Sweetheart, don't start acting all weird on me in front of company. I'm sure I told you about that and many other things."

Though he didn't want to, Isaiah knew to drop the subject. However, he was positive that his mother never told him about any of this.

Brooklyn clutched his arm. "Why don't we go for a walk, too?"

"Why?"

Adrianne Byrd

She tugged as she whispered, "I think they want to spend some time alone."

He stiffened.

She tugged again. "Please."

Still reluctant, he allowed her to help him to his feet. And even as she led him away, he watched his mother and Dr. Ramsey from the corner of his eyes.

Brooklyn couldn't help but find Isaiah's behavior cute. "She'll be fine," she assured him. "I'm sure Dr. Ramsey can take care of her while we're away."

He turned toward Brooklyn and his pensive expression relaxed. "Sorry," he muttered with a sly smile. "I guess I'm handling this badly."

"She never dated after your father died?"

"Off and on." He shrugged. "Nothing that ever became serious."

"So what makes this different?"

Isaiah glanced over his shoulder; his mother was no longer in their line of vision. "I'm not sure."

Brooklyn tugged on his arm and regained his attention.

He smiled down at her. "She likes you though."

"Really?"

He nodded. "A lot."

The thought sent a warm flush throughout her body. Yet, at the same time she didn't understand this need for Georgia's approval. She also didn't understand the dreams she'd been having—about him, Jaleel, and a new baby. Hell, there was even a dog and a white picket fence.

Isaiah draped an arm around her shoulder. "I'm glad we decided to do this."

She smiled as they strolled among the mass of people. "I am, too." She leaned against him and felt at peace with her world. What would the summer have been like had it not been for him? Everything was going great. Her sales were up, her stress level down, and Evan—

"Brooke?"

She stopped cold and her smile faded at the familiar voice.

"Brooke, is that you?"

Slowly, she turned. Dread settled like an iron anchor in the pit of her stomach as she faced a shocked Evan and Macy.

Twenty

"Hello, Evan." Brooklyn's cool voice concealed her shock. Her arm remained draped around Isaiah as she forced one foot in front of the other and moved toward Evan and Macy. "What a surprise. I thought you were going to Lake Lanier."

"Jaleel went with a few of his buddies," Evan answered, but his eyes remained locked on Isaiah. "Nice seeing you again."

Isaiah's arm tightened around Brooklyn's waist. "Likewise."

Brooklyn smiled at the flash of irritation in Evan's face, and then shook her head. Here he was with her ex-best friend on his arm and he had the nerve to appear annoyed.

"Well," Brooklyn said, after a moment of awkward silence. "I guess we should let you get back to what you were doing."

"It was good seeing you again, Macy," Isaiah nodded.

The corners of Macy's mouth lifted but no warmth penetrated her eyes. "Brooklyn, you sly devil," she cooed. "Looks like you're having a good time this summer."

She stiffened in Isaiah's embrace. "I can't complain."

Macy lifted her chin, her anger evident in her hard jawline. "Must be nice having the house all to yourself."

Evan's expression darkened. "I think we should go."

Brooklyn's head filled with snappy retorts, but none were appropriate to say. "Enjoy the rest of your day."

Simultaneously, the couples turned and stalked off in opposite directions.

"Are you all right?" Isaiah asked, after they'd walked for a time.

She flashed him a weak smile. "Never better."

"Liar."

She stopped walking and drew in a deep breath. "Sorry."

"There's no need to apologize." He pulled her into his arms. "And there's no reason why we should let them ruin our day, either." He leaned down and kissed the top of her head.

Warmed by the feel of his kiss and the flash of his smile, Brooklyn nodded. "You're right."

"Of course I am," he said with playful arrogance.

She laughed and leaned into his embrace, where she remained for the duration of their walk.

Before long the day veered back on track and

Brooklyn once again laughed and enjoyed the people around her.

Dusk fell and the much-anticipated fireworks began.

Brooklyn sat contentedly next to Isaiah while she stared up at the array of colors splashed across the sky.

Isaiah's arm fell around her shoulders. When she glanced over at him, his lips brushed against hers in a feathery kiss.

"I'm glad we did this," he whispered.

She leaned into him. "Me, too."

After the show, everyone helped pack and pile everything back into the SUV. But when Georgia announced Paul would take her home, Brooklyn and Toni exchanged knowing looks while Isaiah struggled to remain amiable.

"I think they're cute," Toni said, giving her unsolicited opinion during the ride home. "Gives me hope for the future."

Brian tossed in his two cents. "Yep. Guess they prove that you're never too old."

Isaiah glanced at them in his rearview mirror. "Do you guys mind? You're talking about my mother."

"Oh, come on," Toni droned. "It should warm your heart knowing she has someone to look after her while you're in Texas."

Brooklyn nodded, but hated any talk of Isaiah and Texas.

"I guess you guys have a point," Isaiah admitted grudgingly. "It'll take some getting used to, I guess."

As Brooklyn squeezed his hand, her thoughts wandered to Jaleel's reaction when she introduced him to Isaiah. In no time at all, her temples throbbed at the imaginary explosion.

To pass the time, the small group participated in a game of where-were-you-when as they listened to songs on the "old school" R&B station. The Commodore's "Still" reminded Isaiah of his first heartbreak, while Prince's "I Wanna Be Your Lover" transported Brooklyn back to her first teenage crush.

When Isaiah pulled into the driveway, Brooklyn invited everyone inside.

The foursome brought the food into the house and constructed dinner from leftovers. A box of dominoes was placed on the table and everyone put on their game faces.

By the end of the night, Brooklyn had won three games to Brian's one. The sour faces on Isaiah and Toni were comical at best and truly a Kodak moment.

When Brooklyn and Isaiah walked their friends to the door and said their good-byes, Toni gave Brooklyn a secretive wink. "Have fun and don't do anything I wouldn't."

Brooklyn cocked her head. "That's a very short list." After they were gone, she closed and locked the door. "What a day."

Isaiah leaned down and extracted a kiss before he whispered, "I hope you don't think it's over."

Her body tingled as her head filled with erotic images. "The thought never crossed my mind."

"Good." He kissed her with an undeniable hunger as his hands traveled beneath her shirt.

She moaned softly and ran her hands along the rippled plains of his chest.

While their tongues continued their passionate duel, Isaiah's fingers pinched her erect nipples through the lacy bra. Heat rose and settled in her feminine core as her ache for him increased.

"Let's go upstairs," he whispered.

Not trusting herself to speak, she simply nodded, placed her hand in his, and allowed him to lead the way. When they reached the dining room, she stopped as her gaze fell on the mess they'd left.

Isaiah's body slumped. "Tell you what. I'll clean up down here and you go and take a long bubble bath."

She smiled at the kind thought. "Nah. I can't let you do that. I'll—"

"What did I say?" He turned her chin so she would meet his stare. "I won't be long. Go on upstairs."

She melted beneath his gaze of sincerity. "You certainly know how to spoil a woman."

"I like spoiling you." He kissed the tip of her nose, and then smacked her bottom. "Now get upstairs and I'll see you in a few."

As she climbed the stairs, a broad grin monopolized her face. Inside her bedroom, she sighed. So far, the summer had turned into a dream come true with Isaiah cast as her leading man.

As much as she was enjoying herself, a shiver of foreboding coursed through her. Questions, like how much longer could such a good thing last? and could she handle another broken heart? filled her and weighed heavily on her mind.

Lost in her thoughts, she went into the bathroom and drew her bath. She undressed as the smell of lavender wafted throughout the room. She instantly relaxed when she slid into the hot scented water.

"I can definitely get used to this." She lifted a handful of bubbles and blew them into the air and laughed when they floated around her. Settling against the form-fitted backrest, she closed her eyes and allowed her mind to drift aimlessly.

A loud splash awakened her and she opened her eyes to see Isaiah climbing into the tub. "Mind if I join you?"

"Not at all." She moved to her left to give him more legroom. "Comfy?"

"There're plenty of things we can do in here."

She lifted a curious brow. "Things we haven't done already?"

"We've hardly made a dent on my list." He lifted her foot and gave it a deep massage.

She sank deeper into the tub and closed her eyes. "What are you doing to me?"

"I'm spoiling you. I thought I told you that."

"You might have mentioned it," she said, smiling. His rich laughter deepened her pleasure. As the massage traveled from her feet to her calves, she was convinced she'd died and gone to heaven.

After a long while, his fingers stopped performing their magic and she opened her eyes with a tinge of disappointment.

"Come here," he instructed huskily.

She obeyed and settled herself between his legs.

From the accessory deck, he lifted the top of a crystal dish and removed a bath sponge. He squeezed on a fair amount of liquid soap, and then with smooth, gentle strokes, he washed her back.

When his soapy hands came around to her chest and slid down the valley between her breasts, she leaned against him and submitted to the wondrous feelings his hands provoked. His lips nibbled at her ear as one hand traveled down her taut abs and dipped inside her.

She sucked in a breath and spread her legs. Her moans grew loud and echoed with the room's natural acoustics.

Isaiah rained kisses along her ears, neck, and shoulders. "How are you liking my list?"

"It's a nice list. Mind if I try?" She poured the soap into her hands and rewarded him with some smooth strokes of her own.

"You're a fast learner," he said, pulling her pliant body against him.

"Complaining?"

He kissed her. "Never."

They took their time laughing and playing with the remaining bubbles.

Minutes later, they took turns applying baby oil to their bodies. When Isaiah's hands roamed over her stomach and up toward her breasts, a familiar heat returned.

He lowered her onto the bed. His mouth took the place of his hands to massage the soft bud between her legs. Instantly, she was lost within herself and addicted to this feeling only he aroused.

After a time, the resulting orgasm nearly shot her off the bed.

"Where are you going?" He laughed. "No rules, remember?"

She had no choice but to nod as her chest continued to rise and fall as though she'd completed a marathon.

Isaiah crawled up the bed and reached over into the nightstand jammed with condoms. While he fidgeted with that, Brooklyn took him into her mouth.

His gasp satisfied Brooklyn though she was determined to dangle him over the same edge of insanity. When Isaiah's control cracked, he rolled her onto her back and slid on the condom before he eased inside her.

Their hips moved in a rhythm only they could hear while their moans blended into a duet of passion. When his thrusts became slow grinds, Brooklyn's nails dug deeper into his soft skin.

Her body exploded with a violent shudder and her cry accompanied a fresh stream of tears.

Isaiah growled his release and collapsed in near exhaustion beside her. He pulled her gently against him. "I love you," he whispered as he nuzzled kisses along her neck. "I love you."

Brooklyn stiffened.

Twenty-one

Isaiah sat in the middle of his mother's living room floor trying to superglue a leg back onto a table while he cradled his cell phone on his shoulder. "Hello, Yasmine."

"So you finally remembered how to call someone?" She huffed on the other end. "I was just starting to feel insulted."

Isaiah laughed. "I guess an apology is in order?"

"That or I can introduce you to my good friend Mr. Dial Tone."

"In that case, I'm sorry. I guess time has gotten away from me since I've been in Georgia."

"Six weeks and counting."

"I stopped marking my calendar."

"Uh-huh. Rumor has it you're not coming back." He frowned. "Who said that?"

"I did. The way I see it, you're going to pop the big question to Ms. Hotpants sooner than later."

Isaiah dropped the tube of superglue. "Whoa. No one said anything about marriage."

Yasmine went quiet for a moment, and then asked, "You're in love, right?"

"We already covered this."

"So it stands to reason that you should ask her to marry you. That's the way your mother and I see it, anyway."

He rolled his eyes and continued with his task. "Don't tell me you've been checking up on me through my mother."

"Well, I had to talk to someone. You'd stopped calling."

"Mary isn't keeping you occupied?"

"We broke up," she said in a tone of indifference. "She said something about my job taking up too much of my time. Can you believe it? *Women.*"

"Guess this means you'll be a strong contender for that man of the tear award."

"Woman of the year. I might be one of the boys, but I'm still a woman."

"That's my girl."

"Back to our previous subject." Yasmine's tone turned serious. "When *are* you coming back? Your mother sounds like she's doing great. She's even returning to dance class soon."

"Damn, I'm going to call you Nancy Drew."

"Before you start doing that, why don't you answer my question?"

He shrugged and then answered when he realized she couldn't see him. "I don't know. Maybe I'll stick around till the end of the summer. There's no hurry. Sounds like you have things under control."

"Did you miss my mentioning the death of my social life?"

"You have my condolences."

She sighed. "The things I do for love."

"Thanks, Yas. I owe you one."

"Whatever. Since you're still going to be in Atlanta, I hope you don't mind my crashing with you in August. I have another meeting with Macy Patterson. Looks like we're going to do this merger after all."

"I knew I had the right woman for the job. Of course you can stay here. The more the merrier."

"Who knows, maybe this time I'll finally get to meet this woman who has you whipped."

"Yeah. Who knows?"

"Don't worry, buddy. I won't steal her from you."

Evan's head throbbed mercilessly while he listened to Macy's unfounded ravings about Brooklyn for the umpteenth time. "How many times do I have to tell you I'm not jealous?" he asked.

Macy's cool green eyes narrowed. "Until I believe you," she snapped.

"Keep your voice down," he warned, standing from the bed. "Do you want Jaleel to hear you?"

"Who cares what that little brat hears?"

"Macy," he growled.

"What?" She rounded on him. "Nothing I do for him is good enough. I fix him breakfast and I have to listen to a thirty-minute dissertation of how his mother's cooking is better than mine."

Evan gave a soft nod. He, too, preferred Brooke's down-home cooking to the debacle Macy prepared.

"He'll never accept me as his stepmother. Maybe we should rethink getting married."

"Macy, calm down. He just needs more time to adjust. He'll come around. Trust me."

Her hands settled on her hips. "I'm not happy."

That makes two of us. He stood with his best puppy-dog expression. "What can I do to make this up to you?"

"Other than send Jaleel home?"

His hands fell to his sides as he sighed. "That's not an option. I want to spend time with my son. You knew we were a package deal coming into this."

She crossed her arms and tapped her foot impatiently. "Then you talk to him. I won't stand for his nasty remarks and disrespect any longer."

Evan crossed the room and pulled Macy awkwardly into his arms. "I'll talk to him."

"Promise?"

"Yes. You have my word."

Jaleel pulled his ear away from the door and smirked with satisfaction. Everything was going according to plan. As he tiptoed back to his room, his thoughts turned troubled at the one thing he hadn't counted on: his mother finding a boyfriend.

Toni eased onto one of the stools at the breakfast bar while Brooklyn poured her a steaming cup of coffee.

"So he told you that he loved you. Great. What's the problem?"

Brooklyn exhaled wearily and shook her head. "Haven't you been listening to what I've been telling you? I don't want him to be in love with me. This was supposed to be just a good time, remember?"

Toni shrugged with a blank expression. "Okay, so it's turned into something bigger than that. Roll with it."

Brooklyn returned the pot to the coffeemaker. "I never should have listened to you. I knew from the beginning that nothing good could come of this."

"You're giving me a headache."

"What?"

"Stop trying to control everything. You're acting like you're not getting anything out of the deal. Yes, it was sex in the beginning and now it's something more. Big deal. The man told you that he loved you, *not* that he wants to marry you."

Brooklyn settled her hands on her hips. "And what if he does?"

Toni shrugged. "Do you love him?"

The question knocked Brooklyn off kilter and she struggled not to show it. "That wasn't what I asked you."

"I know, but it's what I'm asking you."

Their gazes met and held for a long time before Brooklyn looked away.

"I don't know if I love him." She grabbed her

coffee cup and joined Toni at the bar. "I don't even know what I'm doing anymore."

"Well, let me tell you what I know," Toni said, swiveling to face her. "I know in the past six weeks, you've been the happiest I've seen in years. How could that be a bad thing?"

Brooklyn lowered her gaze.

"Besides," Toni went on, "what's not to love about the man? He's wonderful and treats you like a queen."

"I know and to tell you the truth that's part of the problem. The man is *too* perfect—other than the fact that he lives a few thousand miles away. Any minute now, I'm expecting this fantasy bubble to pop and find out Isaiah's some raving lunatic who'd escaped from the funny farm or something."

"Oh, give me a break and stop with the excuses." Toni rolled her eyes. "Live it up, take some chances. You're never going to get anywhere if you don't take risks."

"And what if I get hurt again?"

"I'll buy you a box of Band-Aids."

Brooklyn flinched.

Regret lined Toni's face and she drew in a deep breath. "Sorry. That was incredibly insensitive."

"Hmmph. I'm convinced you'd have made a lousy therapist."

"Yeah, but I'm a great lawyer."

They glanced at each other and smiled.

When Brooklyn's gaze fell away, she stared into

her coffee as though waiting for it to show the future. Love? Did she love Isaiah?

"Hello?" Toni probed.

Her trance broken, Brooklyn shook her head and took another sip. "I was just thinking." She then held up a hand to stop whatever smart retort, one-liner, or speech Toni might say. "There're a lot of things to consider. As much as I want to lose myself in this incredible fantasy, there are a lot of things just waiting to crush this relationship."

"Like what?"

"Like Jaleel. He'll be back home next month. How am I going to get him to accept a new man in my life when he's constantly rejecting *me*? Then, there's Isaiah's job. Sooner or later, he's going to have to go back to Texas. And the last thing I want is a long-distance nightmare."

"What does either of those things have to do with whether or not you love the guy?"

Brooklyn drew a blank, and then answered in a low voice, "Nothing."

"Right. Stop getting worked up over nothing. Enjoy him and the precious time you have together while it's still here."

At the end of her friend's speech, Brooklyn's inner turmoil calmed. "I guess you're right."

"Of course I am. How dare you call me a lousy therapist!"

"Going out?" Georgia asked her son from the door of his bedroom.

He turned and looked at her. "I hope you don't mind. But I thought I'd just be the third wheel with Dr. Ramsey coming over."

"Why don't you start calling him Paul?"

Isaiah shrugged. "Habit, I suppose."

She nodded, but her expression said she wasn't buying it. "You know, the good thing about Paul and me is that over the years we've established a solid foundation."

Isaiah smiled while ignoring his discomfort at the direction of their conversation.

"I've always thought it was best to become friends first. Sometimes too much too fast is just that."

His smile waned as his mother's words took root.

As if sensing she'd struck her mark, she winked. "Just think about it," she said.

That night, Brooklyn greeted Isaiah at her front door dressed in a pink silk robe. At his look of surprise, she flashed him a peek of an outrageous thong teddy the color of cotton candy.

Isaiah's jaw dropped.

"See anything you like?" she asked with a playful smile.

"Yes. Every time I see you," he said as he stepped inside and closed the door.

She removed her robe.

"My, my, my," he said as Brooklyn performed a slow pirouette for his approval.

She smiled. "I thought you might like it."

He stepped closer and pulled her into his arms. "I love it." As his head descended, his hand inched through her soft hair. The glorious taste of her instantly muddled his thoughts and his body responded to the power she held over him.

It wasn't until her lips abandoned his to place random kisses along his neck and her fingers tried to make quick work of his shirt's buttons that he was able to think again.

His hand covered her fingers. "No."

Astonishment clouded her eyes. "No?"

He stepped back and flashed a reassuring smile. "It's not that I don't want to. Lord knows it's not that."

"Then what?"

Isaiah reached for the robe she still gripped in her hand and gently placed it around her shoulders. He flinched when embarrassment stained her face. "Maybe I'm going about this the wrong way. Let's go into the living room and talk for a few minutes."

"Talk?"

He nodded. "If that's all right?"

She stared at him as if at a loss for words.

"Come on." He placed his hand beneath her elbow and guided her into the living room.

Not at all happy at how her perfectly planned evening was taking a nosedive, Brooklyn took her seat on the sofa and watched Isaiah with guarded eyes as he sat next to her.

"Okay, so what's up?" she asked.

He drew in a deep breath and looked as though

he didn't know how to begin. For a moment, she thought something bad had happened.

"Come on. What is it?"

He took her hand. "I've been doing some thinking."

Her shoulders sagged as her anxiety deflated. "Thinking?"

He nodded.

"About what?"

"About us."

Suddenly her fear returned. Was he about to call it quits? Was it time for him to go back to Texas? "What about us?" She pulled back her hand.

"I think we got off on the wrong foot."

She blinked, unsure whether she'd heard him right. "What do you mean?"

"I mean—all we do is have sex."

She frowned. "Are you complaining?"

Isaiah shook his head, but then started nodding. "I guess I am. I want more."

"More sex?" she struggled to follow the conversation.

He laughed. "No. I want something more meaningful from you."

"I see," she lied. "Like what?"

"Like love."

She cringed. There was that word again.

"Trust, companionship, and respect," he added. "Everything it takes to build a successful relationship."

"I see," she echoed, unable to think of anything else to say.

Isaiah squeezed her hand, apparently emboldened by her lack of argument. "The first step to see whether we have those other elements is to abstain for a little while."

She blinked. "Come again?"

He nodded. "For at least a couple of weeks."

"No sex for two weeks?" Brooklyn blinked and pulled her robe tighter. "Don't I get a vote on this?"

"I already know how you'd vote."

"Good. My vote cancels out your vote and we can just forget this silly notion." She leaned in for a kiss, but he pulled away.

"Not quite." His expression told her to behave. "We need to do this. Just call it an experiment."

"I'd like to call it crazy." Frustration seeped into her face and voice. "We're great in bed."

"But it's not a solid foundation for a relationship."

She flinched, and then realized her mistake.

"In case, of course, you're not serious about pursuing a relationship." His gaze intensified.

She exhaled and stood from the sofa. "Look, I never lied to you about that."

"And I've never lied to you about what I wanted either."

She walked to the fireplace and turned to face him. "So what do we have—a stalemate?"

"Does the thought of getting serious with me terrify you that much?"

More than you'll ever know. "No."

He laughed. "Liar."

"Okay. Fine. The truth is the thought of being in a relationship with anyone scares the hell out of me."

"Ever?"

She blinked, startled by the question. "I don't know. I haven't thought that far in advance."

"Maybe you should." He stood and walked toward her. "Before I met you, marriage was never in the cards. Now, I think about it all the time."

Her laughter burst from her lungs. "Marriage?" She moved away in order to maintain distance. "Been there, done that, not interested in going back."

"But you've never been married to *me*."

Against her will, his white smile hammered away at her defenses. She closed her eyes and composed herself. "A relationship with you is impossible. You live in another state for crying out loud."

"Look. Knowing you, you can hurl excuses for the rest of the night. I'm just asking you to give me a chance—give us a fair chance. Everything else will take care of itself."

She clamped her jaw tight, not willing or wanting to diffuse her anger.

Meanwhile, Isaiah erased the distance between them with long strides. Before she knew it, he was tilting her chin up so their gazes could meet.

"So what do you say? Are you going to give us a chance?"

She couldn't help but pout. "Two weeks is a long time."

He laughed and kissed her. "I think we'll survive."

Reluctantly, she smiled. "Speak for yourself."

"You never answered my question," he said.

How could she answer him? Where Isaiah was concerned, her mind and body raged an exhausting war every day. How could he believe that sex was the only thing that held them together?

"All right." She held out her hand to seal the deal. "Two weeks."

Isaiah shook her hand.

Then with a mischievous smile, she opened her robe and allowed the silk material to slide from her shoulders. "I guess this means I should change into something more . . . appropriate."

His eyes lowered to her scantily clad figure as she walked past him to head for the staircase.

"Lord, have mercy." He exhaled in a long breath. "You're not going to make this easy, are you?"

She glanced at him from over her shoulder. "Not on your life."

Twenty-two

The next week, August rolled in and Isaiah and Brooklyn were nearly inseparable. Most mornings, after breakfast, he'd pack her a lunch and send her off to work. While she was gone, it left him plenty of time to care for his mother. When Brooklyn returned home, he'd either have prepared dinner or take her out on the town.

However, tonight he had something special planned.

"Ballroom lessons?" she inquired, and then glanced up at the studio he'd parked next to.

He shrugged and flashed her a smile. "You said it was something you'd always wanted to do."

"Y-y-yes. But I meant as a little girl. Sort of like when I told you I used to dream of being a princess."

"Then let's pretend you're a little girl." He unbuckled his seat belt. "But I have to warn you—I'm no Fred Astaire."

Brooklyn gushed with excitement as she watched him get out of the car and walk over to the passenger side. "I can't believe this," she said, stepping out of the car.

Isaiah slid his arm around her waist and kissed the lobe of her ear as he whispered, "How did I do?"

She laughed. "You did great." She leaned against him, relishing the warmth he exuded while they walked into the studio.

"Good evening." A silver-haired Italian woman greeted them at the door. "Are you here for the beginner's class?"

"That would be us," he confirmed and extended his hand. "Isaiah Washington, and this is my girlfriend, Brooklyn Douglas."

Brooklyn smiled. The word "girlfriend" bounced merrily throughout her body as she offered her hand to the smiling woman. "Hello."

"Hi, my name is Cici Castillo. I will be your instructor this evening. If you two would just follow me I'll introduce you to the other couples."

They nodded and obediently followed. Once introduced to the other five couples, they were pleased not to have been the oldest amateurs.

Music filled the studio as Cici took her place before the class. Next to her stood a young male dancer who bore a striking resemblance. She clapped her hands to gain everyone's attention. "For this evening, my dance partner will be my eldest son, Carlos."

Carlos nodded toward the group, and then mother and son faced one another.

"Gentlemen." Cici spoke again. "Traditional etiquette stipulates that the man asks the woman for the dance." She smirked as her head turned toward her group. "I know times have changed and it's perfectly acceptable for women to ask, but since I'm old-fashioned, let's stick to tradition."

A small ripple of laughter coursed through the group.

Cici faced her son again. "Men, bow slightly at the waist and simply ask your partner, 'May I have this dance?'"

Brooklyn's hand fluttered across her heart as Isaiah bowed before her. She nodded and stepped toward him.

Everyone mimicked the instructor's stance as they faced their partners.

With one hand resting on the other's shoulder and their other hand pressed palm-to-palm, Isaiah and Brooklyn watched Cici and Carlos, and then had no trouble gliding in two-four time.

"This isn't so bad," Isaiah said, proudly lifting his chin. "I'm a natural."

"You're something," Brooklyn joked, floating in his arms.

"Ladies." Cici raised her voice above the music. "If you see an oncoming couple about to collide into you and your partner, simply tap your partner gently on the shoulder."

Brooklyn smiled.

"Men, when you receive the signal, *don't* panic. Remain calm and gently guide your partner in the opposite direction."

While everyone whisked around the floor, Cici and her son approached the various couples and adjusted their arm tension: firm wrist, elbow, and shoulder for sideward, forward, and backward movement. Up-and-down motion should be free from resistance.

The two-step slowly became the waltz and Isaiah and Brooklyn were the stars of the class.

"You lied," Brooklyn accused him with a broad smile. "You do know how to dance."

"Trust me, I'm just as surprised as you." Isaiah's eyes twinkled, making it impossible for her to discern the truth.

The rest of their time flew by in a whirl and Brooklyn felt like the belle of the ball and Isaiah her Prince Charming.

After class, they picked up Chinese food instead of keeping their reservations at the upscale Sambuca.

When they arrived at Brooklyn's house, Isaiah reached for a large package from the backseat.

"A present?"

"Maybe." He leaned over, kissed her on the cheek, and then grabbed their dinner.

She battled with guilt and pleasure.

However, Isaiah refused to appease her curiosity. In fact, he seemed quite content to ignore the silver package while they ate their meal in front of the fireplace.

"So, did you have a good time this evening?" Isaiah asked.

Brooklyn's gaze darted away from the package and back to his inquisitive stare. "Yes. I had a wonderful time. Are we actually going to finish the six-week course?"

"Absolutely." He thrust his chin up. "I think I might have missed my calling in life. Don't you think?"

"As a dancer?"

"Yeah. Sure. Why not?"

Brooklyn laughed. "Well, I wouldn't mind seeing you in a pair of tights."

He frowned. "Ballroom dancers don't wear tights."

"Pity." She shrugged and bit into her sesame chicken.

"Of course, you weren't too shabby yourself," he complimented her.

Brooklyn smiled as the memory of their evening played in her mind. "We make a good team."

"It's about time you admit it."

"I was referring to dancing," she informed him with a sarcastic grin.

"I wasn't."

When her eyes met his, her heartbeat quickened. She viewed the wicked glint in his eyes as dangerous. It held an underlying determination that threatened to steal her heart.

"So what's in the box?" she asked, wanting to alleviate the building tension between them.

He shrugged as if it was unimportant. "A gift."

"I figured that much. When do I get to see what's inside?"

He lifted the last of his rice on his chopsticks. "Soon."

Brooklyn resisted the urge to throw something at him. She took the last bite of her food, wiped her mouth, and then crossed her arms. "How soon?"

"Oh, I don't know. How bad do you want to open it?"

She stopped herself from saying she didn't care, mainly because she feared he'd take it back.

"Well?" he asked, carefully examining her expression.

"Can I see what's in the box?"

"First, answer my question."

She gritted her teeth. He'd backed her into a corner. "I'd like to see what's inside the box."

Amusement monopolized his features. "How bad?"

"Bad."

He arched his brows. "Is that all?"

She inched closer and bounced with exaggerated excitement. "Real bad."

He wiped his hands, moved the empty food cartons between them, and grabbed the package to set it beside him. "This gift comes with a price."

Her hands fell to her hips as her gaze narrowed. "What sort of price?"

"I don't know." He shrugged and stroked his chin in thought. "I guess the going rate for gifts is a kiss."

"A kiss?" Her smile returned. "I can handle that." With her hands, she crawled the scant space between them.

When their lips were inches apart, Isaiah placed

his index finger against her lips. "I have to warn you."

Brooklyn stopped with her eyebrows furrowed high above her eyes.

Isaiah chuckled, obviously enjoying his little game. "This can't be an ordinary kiss." He lowered his hand and looped his strong arm around her waist. "This kiss has to be the mother of all kisses."

She laughed but could already feel the army of butterflies swarming inside her. "Talk about pressure."

He shrugged as his smile died away. "Well, if you don't want it." His arm fell from her waist.

She quickly grabbed his arm. "I didn't say that."

A lazy smirk curved the corners of his mouth while his brows jiggled playfully. "Up for the challenge?"

Brooklyn's gaze lowered to his full lips. Their humor vanished beneath the room's sudden sensual intensity. She leaned forward, careful to just brush her lips lightly over his and place a hand over his quickening heartbeat.

Then, as she expected, Isaiah's passion took over and his lips nearly devoured hers.

Her arms slid around his neck and she drew him even closer. Intoxicated by his kiss, the erotic caress of his tongue revived her physical ache.

Their lips parted, but their hold on one another tightened.

Isaiah continued to rain smaller kisses along her neck and the gentle slope of her shoulder.

"How did I do?" she managed to ask between large gulps of air.

"Better than your average bear."

His sexy rumble of laughter filled her ears. She pulled back and settled her weight on her folded knees. "Can I have my gift now?"

"You got it." He picked up the package and presented it to her. "For you, madam."

Never a delicate flower when it came to unwrapping gifts, Brooklyn tore into the beautifully wrapped package and stopped abruptly when she recognized the jeweler's burgundy casing. Her mind raced with possibilities at the box size.

"Aren't you going to open it?" Isaiah inquired, his anxiousness reflected in his voice.

Gently, she opened it and gasped.

Isaiah leaned forward and kissed her. "I hope you like it."

Brooklyn stared openmouthed at the sparkling tiara, unable to pull her eyes away.

Isaiah took the box from her hand and removed it from the velvet interior. "When you told me about your childhood dream, I had no trouble picturing you with this." He slid the small crown onto her head, taking the time to make sure it fit properly.

"I don't believe this," she said, finally recovering from her shock to bubble with laughter.

He stood and reached a hand out to help her up. "How about some music?" He walked over to his jacket he'd draped over the sofa and extracted a CD case. "Let's see if we can put what we've learned tonight to good use."

Seconds later, a slow instrumental filled the room and Isaiah approached her with a slight bow. "May I have this dance?"

"Yes, you may," she answered with a pounding heart. When he took her into her arms, Brooklyn lost herself in his beautiful eyes. She ignored the warnings bells ringing in her head, blocked out her vows of never falling in love again, and just submitted to the magic, which enfolded her whenever she was around Isaiah. Trust this feeling, her heart begged. Trust this man. And God help her, she did just that.

Twenty-three

Isaiah and Brooklyn stepped out of the Atlanta Civic Center arm-in-arm after seeing the Broadway tour of *The Lion King*.

"I have to admit it was better than I expected," Isaiah marveled over the production.

Brooklyn's eyes lit up. "Better than you expected? It was wonderful. I can't thank you enough for bringing me. How on earth did you get tickets on such short notice?"

Infected by her excitement, Isaiah brightened. "Let's just say I have connections."

She leaned into him as she squeezed his arm. "Thank, you, thank you, thank you."

"You really enjoy the theater, don't you?"

"Ever since I can remember. Believe it or not, my mother was an actress once." She laughed softly. "She had visions of being the next Dorothy Dandridge."

His brows rose in surprise. "What happened?"

Brooklyn shrugged. "She met an athlete, fell in love, and had a little girl."

"Any regrets?"

"None that she mentioned. She and my father are still going strong and if you're ever around them, it's like being around two teenagers."

"They sound wonderful."

She nodded. "They are. I'm lucky to have them. It's been hard trying to get down to see them in Florida since . . ."

He glanced at her. "Since the divorce?"

"Yeah."

Smiling, he leaned over and kissed the top of her head. It was important to give her as much support as she needed. It was the only way to conquer the hurdle she kept between them.

They reached his car in the parking lot, two blocks away from the Center and drove to Buckhead, a suburban city of Atlanta.

"So tell me more about your son, Jaleel," he said, glancing over at her in the passenger seat. "He's coming home in a couple of weeks, right?"

"Yeah." She smiled and sighed. "Jaleel is wonderful . . . when he's not angry at me."

"The divorce has been hard on him?"

"Too hard. I'm hoping his time away with his father will help him put things in perspective, but I don't know. Sometimes it seems like he's just bound and determined to blame me for everything."

"How old is he?"

"He'll be seventeen in September."

Isaiah laughed and shook his head. "I can't get over it."

"What?"

"You just don't look like you have a seventeen-year-old son."

"You certainly know the right words to a woman's heart," she said.

"That's good to know." He pulled into the parking lot of The Prime restaurant and turned toward her in his seat. "Have you ever thought about having more children?" Her head jerked toward him and he met her startled gaze with his cool one. "Have you?"

Her mouth moved, but no sound came.

He laughed as he reached over and squeezed her hand. "Don't answer that one." He winked. "I'll ask it at another time." He got out of the car and smiled as he walked over to the other side.

Brooklyn accepted his hand after he'd opened her door.

"You purposely asked me that to throw me off, didn't you?"

"Did I?"

She drew in a breath and then allowed her gaze to fall away.

As they headed toward the restaurant, he slid his arm possessively around her waist. She loved it when he did that and her pleasure only increased when she, too, wrapped her arm around him.

The hostess led them to a secluded table near the back and Brooklyn reveled in the ambience of the dimly lit restaurant.

"So what do you think?" Isaiah asked once they were told the day's specials and handed their menus.

"This is quite cozy. I like it."

"Good. So far I'm two for two."

"Actually, I thought the score was much higher than that." She smiled at seeing the sparkle in his eyes. She leaned forward. "It's a shame."

"What?"

She shrugged with the casual flare of a good actress. "That the night will have to end with a handshake. I'm just dying to express my gratitude for this evening."

His smile faltered as his gaze lowered to her lips. "A handshake might be a bit too formal, don't you think?"

She forced herself to frown and pretended to consider his words. "Mmm. I don't know. We don't want to do anything that might lead to . . . other things."

Isaiah inched to the edge of his seat. "Surely, we can handle a small kiss or peck."

"Can we?"

He nodded and pulled himself erect. "Not to brag, but I handled myself rather well with that knockout teddy you had on last week."

"Oh, you should see the one I have on tonight." She winked.

Isaiah grabbed his glass of water. "You have one on now?"

She nodded. "Red. Your favorite color."

Their waitress appeared and took their drink orders. When they were alone again, Isaiah flashed her a smile.

"You don't play fair."

"Someone told me that all was fair in love and war."

"Are we in love?"

Her smugness evaporated and she was suddenly trapped by her own words. While his eyes leveled with hers, she knew he deserved an honest answer. "I'm not sure."

His hand covered hers and he gave it an affectionate squeeze.

The confession was a strange sort of relief, but at the same time, she was petrified. Despite her protests and denials, something was happening to her—to them—and she was ill-equipped to handle it.

The waitress returned with their wines and scurried off to place their dinner orders.

"Tell me more about your job," she said, desperate to change the subject.

"Okay. What would you like to know?"

"Once upon a time you told me that you were married to it. Is that still true?"

"Not in the past few months."

"And when you leave here?"

"What do you mean?"

She shrugged at his flicker of confusion. "One of the excuses you gave for not being able to commit to your old girlfriend was because you devoted so much time to your career." She held his gaze. "What makes you so sure that it wouldn't happen again?"

"I never felt the desire to give up one thing for another."

"And now?"

"Now I am."

Her skepticism morphed into shock. "You would give up your career for me?"

"Yes."

His answer filled Brooklyn with a new wave of anxiety. Of course, she'd never dream of asking him to do such a thing, but for a moment, she grew heady with the power she held over him.

He gave another squeeze to her hand. "Don't be afraid to love me."

Her eyes moistened. "I can't help it."

He brought her hand to his lips and kissed it. "Then I'm going to do all I can to help you."

During the course of their dinner, the conversation drifted to lighter subjects and Isaiah delighted himself in listening to her laughter. However, the tension returned after he drove her home and walked her to her door.

Brooklyn retrieved her keys from her purse and looked up as she smiled. "I guess this is good night."

His brows rose with surprise. "You're not going to invite me in?"

"Do you think that's wise?"

"I can handle it if you can."

"Is that a challenge?"

He simply smiled and shrugged.

"Okay, Mr. Confident. Why don't you come in for a nightcap?"

"I thought you'd never ask."

She opened the door and he followed her inside.

"I'll get us some wine," she said, and headed to the kitchen.

Isaiah watched the gentle sway of her hips as she walked away. "One week to go," he mumbled, shaking his head. "I must be crazy." He turned and entered the living room.

A few minutes later, she joined him. "Here we are." She extended a wineglass and sat next to him on the sofa.

"Let's make a toast," he said.

"What should we toast to?"

He held his glass to her. "To us."

Her beautiful eyes met his serious gaze while a ghost of a smile danced across her lips. "To us."

They clinked their glasses, and then sipped their wine.

Brooklyn settled against Isaiah and he casually draped his arm around her shoulder. No words were needed, as both were content with their intimate pose.

She could easily get used to this small world they'd created. Who wouldn't want a man who doted on her every word or wish? What would it truly be like to be Mrs. Isaiah Washington?

He kissed the top of her head. "What are you thinking about?"

"You," she whispered as a warm glow radiated from within.

"Anything good?"

"Always. What were you thinking about?"

"The red teddy you have on."

She laughed and tilted her chin so she could look at him. "Ah, ah, ah. Seven more days, lover boy."

He leaned down and kissed her. "Don't remind

me." He kissed her again; his tongue gently delved into her warm mouth.

She moaned softly, her kiss as hungry as his own.

He turned away and a surge of disappointment nearly paralyzed him.

Brooklyn kissed his cheek and silently took their wineglasses and set them on the coffee table. When she curled against him again, her voice held a note of amusement. "Doesn't this remind you of being teenagers and necking on your parents' couch?"

He laughed softly. "My mother would have killed me."

She kissed his chin. "Mine, too, but the possibility of getting caught is part of the thrill." Belatedly, she thought of Jaleel and Theresa and shook her head. "Of course nowadays, teenagers seem to do a little more than just necking."

"Jaleel?"

She nodded. "Trust me. You don't want to hear about it." She dotted kisses along his jaw, and then settled on a sensitive spot just below his earlobe.

Isaiah sucked in his breath and couldn't believe his toes actually curled. "What are you doing?"

"What does it look like?" she whispered.

He quivered from her warm breath against his neck and at the feel of her hand as it slid beneath his shirt. He cursed at their agreement and raked his fingers through her hair. Tugging her head back, he devoured her mouth like a starved man.

His need for her overwhelmed him and he couldn't remember how he'd gotten her dress off.

All he knew now was how incredibly sexy she looked in that damn teddy. He slid the thin straps from her shoulders; his mouth watered at the sight of her full breasts.

He wanted them—wanted her, but he couldn't move.

"What is it?" She looked up at him with passion-filled eyes.

He rolled to her side and monopolized the remaining space on the sofa as he sighed. "We have to stop."

"Why?" Annoyance filled her voice. "I want you and you want me. Why do we have to stop?"

"Because of our agreement."

His answer infuriated her as she pushed herself up and off the sofa. "Fine. I think it's time for you to go." She snatched her dress off the floor and with tremulous hands she jerked the material back on.

"Don't be angry." He sat up and reached for her.

She sidestepped his touch. "Who said I was angry?"

He stood. "It's obvious."

"And it's obvious to me that you're playing games," she snapped back.

"What the hell are you talking about?" he thundered.

"I'm not a toy. You can't just get me all worked up and then shut down."

Isaiah's stare turned incredulous. "I didn't mean . . . we agreed—"

"Spare me the speech about us developing a relationship," she said, refusing to let go of her anger and humiliation. "I never said I wanted a relationship out of this. In fact, I made that clear in New York."

"So what we had this summer meant nothing to you?" He snatched his shirt that had somehow been flung onto the coffee table.

"Of course it did. It meant sex—great sex if you want to stoke your ego."

"Now, who's treating whom like a toy?" he asked in a flat tone while he struggled to hide his bruised pride. He turned with a desperate need to get away before their words became ugly.

Brooklyn's hands dropped to her sides as she watched him storm away. She wouldn't and couldn't say the apology perched on the tip of her tongue. She also refused to follow him to the door. Yet, she jumped at the force of which he slammed it.

At that same instant, her heart leaped into her throat and her vision blurred. She allowed one sniffle and then wiped her eyes clear with the backs of her hands. "I will not cry over another man," she declared adamantly and lifted her chin with a false bravado.

She retrieved the wineglasses and turned out the lights in the living room and then the kitchen. By the time she'd locked up the house and slid into bed, her tears had returned and she was miserable.

"Damn him," Brooklyn moaned into her pillow. Her ache for him wasn't merely physical, but it was mental and spiritual as well. She closed her eyes as tears slid from their corners.

"I don't love him, I don't love him," she chanted in desperation, but her words lacked conviction. This revelation caused her tears to quicken and her sobs to fill her bedroom.

She cried until there were no more tears and she was left to stare at a sliver of moonlight that filtered through her window. Soon, her heartbeat slowed and her jumbled thoughts became easier to comprehend.

When had it happened? How did she get blindsided?

Brooklyn sat up in bed and hugged the pillow. "I'm such a fool," she whispered. "I wasn't supposed to fall in love."

Isaiah had ignored her protests and with small gestures destroyed the well-constructed wall she'd built around her heart.

Whenever he spent the night, she'd awaken to breakfast in bed. Notes of endearments were taped in odd places throughout the house. Twice, he'd showed up at her office and treated her to a picnic lunch in the park. She also loved the time she'd come home to discover a blanket of rose petals that led from the front door to her bedroom where a naked Isaiah lay sprawled across the bed.

Despite her solemn mood, a smile curved her lips. She even loved the time shared during pillow talks. In their short time together, she'd told him everything about her marriage, her friends, life before Evan, and even her childhood fantasies.

Brooklyn laughed as she remembered the tiara he'd purchased and the night he'd dubbed her

Princess Brooklyn. Again, what was there not to love?

Isaiah sat in his mother's living room cloaked in darkness and replayed the night's events in his head. His anger had long left him and he was thinking of ways to salvage what had happened. He still wanted Brooklyn and he was convinced now more than ever that she wanted him, too.

Tonight, she'd tried to push him away—maybe because he'd gotten too close. He smiled at the thought. While she was so busy declaring what she didn't want, he was busy proving her wrong. The bottom line was loving Brooklyn came easy to him.

"What are you doing sitting alone in the dark?" Georgia asked, clicking the light on from behind him.

"I was just thinking." Isaiah glanced over his shoulder and watched as she entered the room. "Is there something I can get for you?"

She waved off his question and settled in the armchair across from him. "I'm fine. I want to hear what's got you thinking so hard."

"Brooklyn." He shrugged as if the answer should have been obvious. "We sort of had a little fight this evening."

"Sort of? Little fight?" She laughed. "Honey, either you did or didn't. Which is it?"

As usual, his mother's directness unarmed him. "Okay. We had a fight."

"Serious?"

"Nah. I don't think so. In fact, I'm thinking about driving back over there."

His mother nodded. "A couple should never go to bed angry. That was something your father and I strongly believed in." She folded her arms and studied him. "You love her, don't you?"

His smile turned sly. "More than anything."

"It does my heart good to hear you say that," she said, and nodded toward the door. "Go talk to her."

Isaiah stood, walked over to his mother, and then kissed her gently on her forehead. "Thanks, Mom."

Brooklyn picked up the phone to call Isaiah when the doorbell rang.

"He's back," she gushed as she threw back the covers, grabbed her robe, and rushed down the stairs. The grandfather clock chimed one A.M. as she fumbled with the locks and threw back the door, ready to apologize.

However, the stoic face that greeted her was the last person she'd expected to see.

"Evan, what are you doing here?"

Twenty-four

Evan shoved his hands into his pants pockets and flashed her an uneven smile. "Hello, Brooke."

A warm breeze ruffled the hem of her robe. She remembered what little she had on and tightened her belt. "Is something wrong? Where is Jaleel?"

"Oh, he's fine. Probably sleeping like a baby back at the house."

Brooklyn remained confused and cautious at his strange behavior. "Then what—"

"Aren't you going to invite me in?"

Something must be wrong, she reasoned before allowing him to enter. "Come in."

Evan crossed the threshold and she closed the door behind him. Folding her arms across her chest, she waited for an explanation. She took in his disheveled appearance and absently wondered when he last had a full night's sleep.

Evan's gaze dragged slowly over her appearance and finally he smiled as though she'd passed his inspection. "You look great."

Her gaze narrowed while her irritation stiffened

her back. "Surely, you didn't drive across town to tell me that."

His smile turned sheepish as he shook his head. "No, I guess I didn't," he admitted, but he still hesitated in giving an explanation. "Can we go in and sit down?"

Her impatience snapped. "*What* are you doing here?"

He shrugged, but his cheesy smile thinned. "I want . . . need to talk with you."

She weighed giving him a few minutes of her time versus kicking his sorry butt out. In fact, the scales had tilted toward the latter when he broke into her thoughts.

"That's if you're not busy." He glanced toward the stairs and back at her.

Her hands fell to her hips. "Maybe I am and maybe I'm not. What difference does it make?" She pivoted toward the door, her tolerance for games maxed out. "Go home."

He rushed forward and placed his hand against the door to prevent her from opening it. "Brooke, I'm sorry. I had no right to ask."

She glanced up at him and was shocked by his look and sound of desperation.

Evan drew in a breath as his shoulders slumped. "Can we *please* sit and talk for a little while?"

It had been a long time since she'd seen this side of her ex-husband. So long, in fact, that she was taken completely off guard and was unsure of what to say. She stepped away from the door and once again folded her arms.

"Please?"

Her gaze met his and lingered for a long moment before she finally nodded.

"Thanks."

Brooklyn set aside her anger, pain, and distrust. "I guess we can talk in the living room." She turned and led the way. As she came around the sofa, she clicked on the lamps on the end tables.

Evan waited until she sat down before he took the space next to her and flashed her another sheepish smile.

"All right." She folded her hands in her lap. "I'm listening."

He nodded and seemed to struggle with where to begin.

"Evan, you're scaring me. If something is wrong, just spit it out. I can handle it."

"Nothing's wrong, Brooke. I mean, something is wrong, but it's not what you think. Actually, I don't know what you're thinking."

"You're rambling."

He stopped and closed his eyes as he drew in another breath. "Sorry."

She flashed him a genuine smile. "It's okay."

Another deep breath and he tried again. "I owe you the biggest apology."

He captured her full attention and she settled back against the sofa and waited.

"I know I'm to blame for the failure of our marriage. I realize now that I was wrong for a lot of things."

Brooklyn rolled her eyes, convinced that the

two sentences were about all she could stomach. "Please tell me you didn't come over here to tell me this."

When he couldn't meet her stare, she laughed with disbelief. "Okay, fine. It was your fault. Thanks for the confirmation." She went to get up.

Evan placed a hand on her arm. "Hear me out."

She stayed put against her better judgment.

"Macy and I were a mistake," he said, finally meeting her gaze. "I know that now."

Had she heard him right?

"Brooke." He took hold of her hand. "I know what I'm about to ask you might come as a surprise, but I'd appreciate it if you wouldn't given me an answer tonight. I want you to really think it over." He brought her hand up and placed it against his heart. "Think about our twenty-year history and give me an honest answer."

"She left you, didn't she?" She snatched her hand away. It was the only thing she could come up with. His hesitation was her answer. She laughed and shook her head. "This is so pathetic."

"Brooke—"

She held up a hand to shut him up. "So what's this really about? You're afraid of being alone?"

"No," he insisted in a firm voice. "She didn't leave me . . . exactly."

"Well, you *exactly* left me or am I supposed to forget that?"

"Of course not," he said, managing to look contrite and amazingly close to tears. "I made a mistake."

"You're damn right you did," she snapped.

"Brooke, can we please set aside the anger?" He met and held her sharp gaze. "I don't know what got into me or what I thought I was searching for. And tonight I realized I had what I wanted all along with you . . . and our son."

"Evan—"

He took her hand again. "I want to come back. I want to give our marriage another try." He inched closer, squeezing her hand. "Will you give me another chance?"

"I hope I didn't catch you two at a bad time."

Brooklyn and Evan jumped up, startled by the intrusion of another voice.

When her eyes landed on Isaiah's crushed expression and the bundle of carnations at his side, her heart plummeted.

Guilt blazed through Brooklyn as her gaze swung between the two men. It also took her a full minute to realize they were waiting for her to say something.

"Evan just came over to talk . . . I'm sure this looks a little odd." A smile fluttered weakly at her lips and she wasn't sure whether she was helping or tossing gasoline onto a fire.

"It's a little odd," Isaiah agreed and folded his arms in front of him as his gaze now swung to Evan. "We meet again."

Evan darkened, not bothering to mask his anger or jealousy.

Both men held their posts, waiting for the other

to make his exit. Brooklyn realized she'd have to ask one of them to leave.

She turned toward Evan. "I'll definitely give it some thought." She glanced at Isaiah, and then back at her ex-husband. "I'll call you."

Evan's jaw hardened while his eyes resembled black steel. However, Brooklyn experienced a rush of relief when he just nodded and moved quietly out of the living room.

With slumped shoulders, she deserted Isaiah and followed Evan to the door.

When Evan crossed the threshold, he stopped and turned back toward Brooklyn. Gone was any evidence of his previous anger. "How serious is it between you two?"

A residue of pain stained his question and she understood how much it cost his pride to ask.

"You lost the right to ask a long time ago," she answered in a low voice.

His gaze met hers and she was surprised by its sparkling sheen. "I ruined the best thing that ever happened to me, didn't I?"

"The best thing that ever happened to us." She pressed her lips together to prevent herself from saying more.

He nodded and lowered his gaze before making his final plea. "Think it over, Brooklyn." He turned and stalked off toward his car.

She watched him, and then slowly closed the door.

Emotionally exhausted, she walked back into the living room and glanced up at Isaiah.

He said nothing as he studied her. Slowly, a smile flickered at the corners of his mouth. He set the bundle of carnations down on a nearby end table, and then opened his arms.

She went to him and buried herself against his chest. His embrace, his scent—*he* felt like home. This was where she belonged.

A Slice of Reality

Twenty-five

Exactly seven nights later, two weeks since Isaiah and Brooklyn's self-imposed torment, the sex-starved couple dove into bed at the stroke of midnight. Eager hands tore at each other's clothes as hot lips raced to reclaim familiar territory.

At times their fervor resulted in fumbles and awkward positions, which both handled with tolerance and laughter. Soon enough, their bodies found their rhythm and their passionate lovemaking elevated them to a plane that only existed in paradise.

Hours later, while Brooklyn slept peacefully, Isaiah came to a decision. He smiled in the fading darkness, and then fell asleep next to the woman he loved.

When he finally opened his eyes, sunlight flooded the room and the space beside him was empty. The clock next to the bed read ten o'clock and he was amazed he'd overslept. Brooklyn had undoubtedly left for work hours ago.

A hot shower revived him before he made a

quick breakfast of eggs and toast, and then rushed out with a clear destination in mind.

Nancy, the sales associate at Opulence, remembered Isaiah from his tiara purchase and greeted him with a smile.

"I'm looking for the perfect engagement ring," he announced with a boastful smile.

"Then you've come to the right place," she said and escorted him to a private area. He had a clear image of what he wanted and Nancy listened intensely before she disappeared. When she returned with two associates and six trays of magnificent emerald-cut diamond rings, Isaiah felt like a kid in a toy store.

The afternoon flew by as he studied and compared each ring through a 10x loupe. Through it all, Nancy exhibited the patience of Job, while he fussed over carat, cut, color, and clarity.

Just when he thought all hope was lost, he found it: a ring that stole his breath and won an enormous smile from Nancy.

"No woman could say no to that ring," she said as he handed over his credit card.

"Let's hope you're right."

Brooklyn didn't go to work. Instead she spent the day driving around Atlanta visiting nostalgic places such as the church where she'd married Evan, Grady Hospital where Jaleel had been born, and even Emory Hospital, which had been Evan's second home during the early years of their marriage.

Wasn't it just yesterday when Evan proposed in her parent's kitchen or when Jaleel took his first steps? No. Yesterday was when Evan broke her heart and walked out on their eighteen-year marriage.

But, when did she meet the tall, gray-eyed Isaiah who mended the shattered pieces? When did she let him into her life and, Lord, when did she start loving him?

She watched the sunset over the sea of cars on the interstate. "I can't do this again," she whispered, though her words had no effect on her heart. *"Why* am I doing this again?"

Evan's woeful expression floated to the surface. He wanted her back. She gave a half laugh and shook her head. He put her through hell, popped up with an age-old excuse of "he didn't know what had come over him," and expected her to welcome him back with open arms.

To add pressure, Evan had contacted her mother and made his plea known. Her parents, dismayed by their divorce, had renewed hope and were actively trying to put her family back together again. But her parents didn't know about Isaiah.

Attentive, beautiful, and caring Isaiah.

Would he ever break her heart?

Brooklyn grew frustrated trying to predict the future as she inched along the freeway. Dealing with questions on whether it was too soon to jump back into a relationship, or how Jaleel would react, elevated her headache to a full migraine.

By the time she pulled into her driveway, she had forced her troubled thoughts into the background and concentrated on what to prepare for dinner. With the summer slowly drawing to a close, the remaining time she had with Isaiah should be special.

A night on the town held some appeal but, frankly, she didn't want to share him with the world. Tuesday night dance classes were enough.

Once inside, she spent three hours preparing a special Italian dinner in between loading clothes in the washer before she rushed upstairs to get ready. Wonderful memories of her and Isaiah making love swirled inside her head and brought a smile to her face as she moved from room to room.

In the shower, one thing certainly became clear: She didn't just merely love Isaiah. She was *in* love with him. Her hands stilled on her body as she let the realization sink in, and then an incredulous laughter bubbled and echoed off the tile.

Later that evening, Isaiah arrived at Brooklyn's house dressed in gray khaki slacks and a loose gray pullover. His clothes selection had taken twice his normal time. To show up in his finest would pique Brooklyn's curiosity, so he decided to keep it casual.

He slid his hand into his pocket and fumbled with the jewelry box before he entered the house.

Brooklyn descended the stairs like a breath of fresh air. Dressed in jeans and a red V-neck top, she made him feel as though he'd overdressed.

"Don't you look nice," she complimented him

as she walked up to him and brushed a kiss against his cheek. "I hope you're hungry. I made dinner."

So much for the reservations he'd made. "Great," he said and heard his own anxiousness in his voice.

Her brows furrowed, but her smile remained sincere. "Are you all right?"

He shrugged and tried to play it cool, but his acting skills were questionable at best. "So, what are we having?"

Her suspicious expression lingered for a second longer, and then she, too, shrugged. "Veal Sorrentino."

"Mmm. It smells and sounds wonderful." He slid an arm around her waist and placed a kiss on top of her head. He'd propose after dinner, he decided, and another wave of nervousness washed over him. "When do we dig in?"

"No time like the present."

The phone rang and Isaiah frowned when he felt Brooklyn tense. "Problem?"

A strange smile fluttered to her lips. "Nah. I'll answer it. Do you mind getting the plates and glasses down for me?"

"Not at all."

Brooklyn headed to the living room while Isaiah went into the kitchen. The caller ID displayed her parents' name and phone number, and her energy rushed from her body with a dramatic sigh.

"Hello, Mom." On the other end, her mother sounded quite the opposite: bubbly, vibrant. "Yes. I got your two messages," she whispered and checked around to make sure Isaiah didn't sneak up on her. "I can't talk about this now. I have company."

Isaiah's head jutted from around the corner. "Red or white wine?" he asked.

"White," she answered, and then focused her attention back on her mother. "No. I wasn't talking to you. Yes. I have a date and no, it's not with Evan." Her mother's sudden gasp and then silence put her on edge. "Can we just talk about this later?"

Her mother bent her ear for a few more minutes, clearly unhappy about what she'd just learned. Brooklyn was finally successful in getting her off the phone.

"Is everything all right?" Isaiah asked when she finally joined him in the dining room.

"Never better," she assured him with a fake smile.

During the course of their meal, Brooklyn allowed the world outside her door to fade. All that mattered now was the man across from her.

Isaiah hardly tasted his meal. He was too busy trying to figure out a way to work his proposal into the conversation. It was customary to propose on bended knee, that much he knew, but nothing else.

He'd heard of proposals where the man slipped the ring into the woman's wineglass, but he instantly had horrible images of the thing being swallowed and the evening ending with a trip to the emergency room—definitely not a good idea.

"I rented a movie," she said, standing from the table and collecting their plates.

"Oh?" He stood and helped clear the table,

while his thoughts circled around the weight in his pocket.

"Hello. Anybody home?" Brooklyn waved a hand in front of his face.

Embarrassed, he laughed. "I'm sorry. What did you say?"

"Only that I won fifty million dollars in the Georgia lottery and I'm moving to Brazil."

"That's great. How about we go into the living room? I'll bring some more wine."

She laughed as she stared at him. "Something is definitely up with you." She crossed her arms. "Out with it."

He tried to blink the confusion from his eyes. "What makes you say something's wrong? I just wanted to just spend some quiet time with you."

Her expression remained the same. "Uh-huh."

He retreated farther into the kitchen and grabbed another bottle of wine. "All right. I have something I want to talk to you about."

"Is it serious?" she asked worriedly.

This time his smile came easy. "I'd like to think so." He moved closer and brushed another kiss against her forehead.

Together they walked into the living room and settled on the sofa.

Isaiah's heart pounded hard in his rib cage as she looked up at him with anxious eyes. The space between them intensified and he was unable to re-call any of the speech he'd practiced for the better part of the day.

"Are you trying to tell me you're going back to Texas?" she guessed.

Isaiah's heart melted at the sadness edging her eyes. Yet, that same emotion gave him hope.

"No. I'm not leaving. That's something else I'll have to address, but not now."

She exhaled and relief deflated her posture. "Then what is it?"

The phone rang and they both groaned.

Brooklyn started to get up.

"Don't answer it," Isaiah said, wanting to get this moment over with before he had a heart attack.

"I have to." She patted his arm. "It might be Jaleel." She stood and walked over to the phone by the door of the living room. "Hello."

Meanwhile, Isaiah dropped his head into the palm of his hand and closed his eyes as he mouthed the words "will you marry me" in a test run.

"Oh, my God," Brooklyn gasped.

Isaiah jerked his head toward her as she fluttered a hand over her mouth. Instantly, he jumped to his feet.

In the next second, tears slid from her eyes as she looked up at him and said, "Jaleel has been in an accident."

Twenty-six

Isaiah drove Brooklyn to Gwinnett Hospital. The trip passed in a blur as the sound of Evan's horror-laden voice echoed incessantly in her head while a steady stream of tears poured from her eyes.

"He bought him a Jet Ski," she said, shaking her head.

"He's going to be all right." Isaiah slid his free hand over to grasp her cold, clasped ones.

She squeezed her eyes closed and clung to his declaration. The last time she'd spoken to her son had been two nights ago when he'd made his anger clear that she hadn't accepted Evan back with open arms.

She, too, had been angry and, once again, allowed her temper to get the best of her. The frustration of her family trying to force her back into a life she didn't want made her lash out at the wrong person. Now, regret suffocated her.

Opening her eyes, she turned and stared out her side window, but saw nothing.

Isaiah glanced at her and took note of how she seemed to shrink before his eyes. They parked outside of the emergency room, and then rushed inside together. In the waiting room, they found a devastated Evan slumped in a chair.

"Evan?"

He lifted his head, his features twisted into a mask of misery that humbled Isaiah.

"Brooke?" Evan's voice cracked beneath the weight of the world pressed against his shoulders.

When Brooklyn moved from Isaiah's possessive embrace and crossed over to the arms of her ex-husband, something tugged inside Isaiah.

He moved to the nearest chair to avoid intruding on their privacy.

"What are the doctors saying?" Brooklyn asked, her voice a replica of Evan's.

"Samuel hasn't been out here. They're still in the operating room."

"Have you been in?"

"They won't let me." His bloodshot eyes held hers. "It's bad, Brooke."

She closed her eyes and fought like hell to block the horrific images surfacing in her mind. "He's going to be all right," she reinforced, though the words lacked conviction.

She reopened her eyes when Evan's arms fell away. His gaze had now discovered Isaiah and she was ashamed to realize that she'd forgotten him.

Evan said nothing as he refocused his attention on her and shoved his hands into his pockets. "This is all my fault." His whispered confession just barely reached her ears.

"What happened?"

"I should've listened to you and never bought him that damn Jet Ski, but I was looking for ways for us to bond. Lord knows I don't spend enough time with him. Even this summer the only thing we did was that two-week camping trip in June. Other than that, he spent more time with Macy than he did with me."

Brooklyn stiffened.

Evan shook his head. "Sorry. I shouldn't have brought her up."

She expelled a long breath. She didn't want to fight. Fighting never solved their problems—no sense in believing now would be any different.

"What happened?" she asked again, trying to keep her impatience at bay.

"It was just a little after sunset, we were out on the lake, he was speeding . . . I kept telling him not to get too close to the boats and to practice courtesy on the water."

Evan was trying either to pacify her or shift blame. She was unsure of which, but she continued to wait for the full story.

"Where were you during all of this?"

"I was riding, too, but was quite a ways behind him."

The truth struck her. "Were you racing him?"

Evan squeezed his eyes shut and she got her answer. "Th-then what happened?"

"I don't think he saw the boat. I know I don't recall seeing it, but suddenly the boat was right on him." Evan's body trembled as his voice croaked. "He tried to turn, but it was too late."

Brooklyn turned away from him to wrestle with her grief as Evan relayed the extent of Jaleel's injuries.

For more than an hour, the three parties occupied three different sections of the waiting room. None of them wanted to trespass on the others' space or impose on their thoughts.

Brooklyn shattered the stalemate and sank in the chair next to Isaiah.

His arm instantly draped around her shoulder and pulled her close.

She drew comfort from his warmth and his underlying strength. He was her rock—that much was as clear as the air she breathed. Fresh tears trickled over her lashes, but by some strange miracle she didn't collapse in the emotional whirlpool around her.

Another hour passed and finally Dr. Samuel Aguilera made his first appearance in the waiting room; his expression was as somber as their own.

Evan crossed the room to his colleague. Brooklyn and Isaiah closed in behind them.

"Just give it to us straight," Evan directed with bated breath.

"He's out of surgery and is being moved to ICU," Samuel began gravely.

Brooklyn squeezed Isaiah's hand as a ripple of hope coursed through her.

"He's still in critical condition . . . and he's in a coma."

Brooklyn slumped back against Isaiah.

"Oh, my God," Evan muttered.

"When can we see him?" she asked.

"Give us a few more minutes to get him situated, and then we'll take you to his room." He flashed them an uncertain smile and then vanished.

Evan turned toward Brooklyn and for the second time that night, she abandoned the safety of Isaiah's arms to embrace her ex-husband.

Isaiah understood, but his heart broke all the same.

Time crawled at a snail's pace and after a week there had been no change in Jaleel's condition. Both sets of grandparents arrived and everyone tried to encourage one another. Mother and father held vigil day and night, while Isaiah faded more into the background.

Then one morning, Isaiah arrived at Jaleel's room and overheard Brooklyn and her mother.

"Evan needs you right now," Karen, Brooklyn's mother, said with a note of authority. "Surely, you see that."

Brooklyn didn't answer.

"Look, sweetheart. I know that whole business with him and Macy is still a sore issue with you and I understand. But sometimes men do things that . . . well, just sometimes they don't think. They reach a certain age—"

"Mom, I don't want to talk about this right now."

"But you need to think about it," Karen insisted. "I know you still love him. He's the father of your child. You have too much time invested to just throw it away."

"Did Dad ever suffer from midlife crisis?"

Karen didn't answer.

"Mom?"

Her mother drew in a deep breath. "Do you remember when you were eight years old and you got to spend the summer with your grandparents?"

"Y-yes."

"Well, your father and I came very close to getting a divorce. He had an affair with a woman who'd fallen in love with him. I didn't know about it until one day she called to tell me."

"I don't believe this. Why didn't you tell me this before?"

"You were too young. But I'm telling you now because I know what you're going through. Your father made a mistake and we were able to work through it. I think you and Evan can do the same."

Isaiah turned and left the hospital.

As another week passed, Georgia tried her best to keep her son's spirits up, but life had sliced him a piece of reality he couldn't fully comprehend. At the hospital, he'd watched the bond between Evan and Brooklyn strengthen and he didn't know how to handle his growing jealousy.

"Why do you have to go back to Austin?" Georgia asked, watching as he packed.

"I'm not helping anyone by staying here," he answered, careful to avoid eye contact. "You're doing great, and Brooklyn . . . has to take care of her family right now. I've run out of excuses to stay."

"This is a difficult time for her."

"I understand that, Mom. I'm not blaming her. I'm not angry." He released a frustrated sigh at the obvious lie. "The first time Brooklyn and I met, she told me a relationship was impossible and, like an idiot, I ignored her. I was so sure I could change her mind—bend her to my will, you might say. Now, the truth is too big to ignore."

"You think she's still in love with her ex-husband?"

He closed his eyes in an effort to block out the pain of the possibility. It didn't work. "I don't know."

Georgia crossed the room, but he still refused to look at her. He didn't want her to see his pain.

"Talk to her."

He gave a tired laugh. "Don't you think that would sound a little selfish right now—considering the circumstances? She might lose her son and I'm whining about my hurt feelings."

"Then you need to stay. Wait till this storm passes."

Isaiah shook his head, his mind made up. "I didn't go to the hospital yesterday," he confessed. "I got tied up doing some errands around here."

"Those could have waited."

He shook his head. "Brooklyn never called to give any status reports. I doubt she noticed I wasn't there." He caught how his voice quivered and then forced resolve back into his tone. "I've put my life on hold long enough. Brooklyn is where she needs to be." The memory of Evan asking Brooklyn to take him back kept resurfacing. They had a twenty-year history and a teenage son—how could he compete with that?

Georgia grabbed his hand and recaptured his attention. "I wish you would reconsider."

He ignored the stinging in his eyes and the hollow ache in his heart. "It's over."

Brooklyn sat beside her son's bed in the ICU, content to just stare at his still form. Their fights in the past year vanished from her memory. All she remembered now was the laughter of his childhood. In the past two weeks, she could remember every birthday, sporting event, and Christmas with remarkable clarity.

Her promises to God for Jaleel to open his eyes grew wild and more desperate with each minute. When her prayers went unanswered, her pain intensified while an endless river of tears fell from her eyes.

Across the room, Evan wrestled with his own demons.

As much as Brooklyn wanted to ease his burden, she couldn't. Just as she couldn't silence the voice within that also blamed him for their son's accident.

She had difficulty accepting solace from her own parents, despite their good intentions. Their insistent mantra for Evan and Brooklyn to put aside their differences and become a family again rode her last nerve.

To believe them was to believe Jaleel's accident was punishment for the failure of their marriage. She refused to accept that—just as she refused to accept that she'd lose Jaleel.

She stood from her chair and kissed her son's warm cheek. "It's time to wake up now," she urged softly and took his hand.

Jaleel didn't move.

Closing her eyes, she allowed sorrow to rule over her emotions.

Evan placed a hand against her shoulder, and without thinking, she shrugged it off. She wanted him to leave them alone. That's what he wanted to do two years ago—why should now be any different?

"Brooke, why don't you take a break?" he asked.

She ignored the hurt in his voice while she struggled with the desire to punish him.

"Brooke?"

"I don't need a break," she said, her voice edgy.

Silence stretched between them before Evan spoke. "Don't do this."

There was no point feigning ignorance, she knew exactly what he meant. He didn't want to fight, but she did—no matter how pointless.

Then she felt it. The tiniest squeeze to her hand. "Jaleel?" she asked. Her eyes widened in surprise.

"What is it?" Evan asked, inching closer.

"He moved." She glanced down at her hand and wondered if she'd imagined it. Then he squeezed again.

"I saw it," Evan exclaimed with a thunder of incredulity.

Slowly, Jaleel's eyelids fluttered open.

A rush of tears flowed down his parents' faces as Jaleel's eyes sharpened with recognition and an awkward smile lifted the corners of his mouth.

"Hi, Mom."

Twenty-seven

A week later, Brooklyn arrived home exhausted. Her mother had finally convinced her to go home and get a full eight hours of sleep. As Brooklyn entered the house, images of having one of Isaiah's famous massages brought an instant smile to her face.

Come to think of it, she wouldn't mind if he did a few other things to help her relax. Opening the door to her bedroom, she felt as if it had been aeons since she'd last been there. Since the accident, her brief visits home usually consisted of her sleeping in Jaleel's room. Tonight, however, she'd sleep in her own bed.

She made a beeline to the bathroom and peeled off her clothes. In the shower, her thoughts returned to Isaiah. She definitely needed to see him tonight. It had been too long.

She frowned as her hands stilled on her body. Just how long had it been? She searched her memory and honestly couldn't remember.

Quickly, she rinsed off, grabbed a nearby towel, and draped it around her as she made a mad dash out of the shower. Had something happened to Georgia?

She struggled to ward off a rising panic and paid no heed to the trail of water she dripped across her bedroom. She reached for the phone and dropped down onto the edge of the bed, and then jumped back up when something crinkled beneath her. Turning, she stopped cold at the sight of an envelope with her name written in Isaiah's unmistakable penmanship.

After a full minute, the erratic pounding of her heart slowly died, just long enough for her to gather her courage, reach for the envelope, and open it.

Dear Brooklyn.

I love you. It's important for me to tell you this first and foremost. But over the past week, I've concluded that my loving you might not be enough. For the first time, it has become clear that there's no room in your life for me. Our summer affair has been wonderful, but what happens when Jaleel returns and Evan wants you back again? He loves you—you'd have to be blind not to see that. My heart goes out to you and your family in your time of need and I'll keep Jaleel in my prayers. But seeing you with your family, I understand your reasoning for why a relationship with me is impossible. Whenever you're with your family, I see something I can never be a part of and to be honest, I'm jealous. I'm jealous of every part of your life that doesn't include me and I'm hurt by your in-

sistence on keeping me out. Could it be because your
heart still belongs to Evan? I love you . . . enough
to let you be happy with someone else.

> *Sincerely yours,*
> *Isaiah*

Brooklyn blinked as the letter slipped through
her trembling fingers.

He was gone.

Jaleel never planned his accident, and he definitely wouldn't recommend it as a course of action
to get one's parents back together. At first he
couldn't argue with the unexpected results. Now,
he wasn't so sure. His parents visited him every
day, but as the days passed, he noticed they'd
started coming in shifts.

Despite his mother's insistence that nothing was
wrong, Jaleel sensed her sadness. Sometimes when
she thought he was asleep, he'd watch her stare
out of his hospital window as if she was waiting for
someone to return. A few times, he'd even caught
her crying. It was at those times when it became
difficult to cling to his selfish desires.

Since the accident, Jaleel couldn't explain his
change of heart. Yes, he'd love it if his parents
were able to get back together, but he no longer
wanted it at any cost. Certainly not at the expense
of his mother's tears.

* * *

During the month of October, Isaiah and Yasmine zipped across the United States for one business meeting after another. The hectic schedule was meant to keep Isaiah's mind off Brooklyn Douglas, despite what he told his friends.

That is until the morning Yasmine quit.

"What do you mean you quit?" Isaiah thundered, staring up at her from his desk. "I need you to go to Hong Kong this Saturday."

Randall cleared his throat, but the tension in the room remained thick.

Yasmine tossed the folders from her hand onto Isaiah's desk, and then jammed her fists into her sides. "Look, if you want to kill yourself—fine. But I'll be damned if I'll let you kill me, too. I need a day off. I need a life outside of Rotech—and so do you."

"I've had three months off."

She clapped. "Good for you. While you were off re-creating *9½ Weeks,* we were here busting our butts." She gestured to Randall.

"Fine. I'll go alone. Take the week off and come back with a better attitude."

She slapped her hands onto his desk as she leaned in. "Who do you think you're talking to?" she snapped.

Isaiah's retort crested his tongue but died when he grabbed hold of his anger. Instead, he clenched his jaw and forced himself to lower his glare. "I was out of line."

Yasmine pulled herself erect. "Why don't you just call her? Make the rest of our lives easier."

Flinging his pen onto his desk, he leaned back in his chair and risked meeting her stare. "We agreed not to talk about this."

"I never agreed to such a thing. I did, however, elect to let you try to work this one out on your own, but since you're not using the good sense God gave you, it's time I helped you."

"I don't need help—from either of you." His sharp gaze swung to Randall just as he was opening his mouth to comment.

"You need something—a pill, a drink, God— something." She moved to the empty chair across from his desk. "If you won't talk to her then talk to me. I'm your best friend, remember?"

Their stares held for an indeterminable amount of time before Isaiah looked away. "I did the right thing, Yas. For both of us."

She stared at him while she chose her words carefully. "Let me tell you what I know." She crossed her arms. "I know you're in love with Brooklyn. I hear it in your voice. I see it in your actions. You walked away to prove how much you love her. You want her to be happy, even if it's not with you. It's the same thing you did with Cadence."

"I think your memory is a little off." Randall successfully jumped into the conversation. "Cadence left him, remember?"

"And he didn't fight for her either. I *expected* him to fight for Brooklyn."

"I'm still in the room, you know." Isaiah popped up from his chair and walked over to his wide view of downtown Austin. "Brooklyn isn't some business acquisition I can wrestle and win with smooth words and a politician's smile. I thought so, at first. I thought if I did everything right, I could tear down that damn wall she built between us."

"Don't you think you did that?" Yasmine asked.

Isaiah closed his eyes and in his mind saw the diamond ring he kept in his briefcase. "I thought I did."

Randall shook his head. "Your walking away was either admirable or foolish."

Isaiah tensed.

"Foolish because it's a gamble," Randall continued. "You're hoping that she'll pick up the phone and beg you to come back. Not simply call and leave updated reports on her son and noncommittal chatter about wanting to talk, but to lay it on the line and say that she chooses you over her ex-husband."

"Refusing to play first runner-up is foolish?"

Yasmine moved toward him. "It is when you don't tell her that's what you're doing. You're hoping she'll figure it out."

He opened his eyes and turned to face them. "Did I tell you that her husband asked to come back?"

Yasmine blinked. "What?"

"Come again?" Randall said.

He shrugged. "To be honest, it didn't worry me too much. Call it arrogance."

"Did she?"

"I don't know." He shrugged again. "But when I saw them together at the hospital, suddenly there was something there I never saw before—an invisible bond, perfectly intact."

Yasmine stood and joined him at the window. "You left her before she could leave you, didn't you?"

Isaiah shifted beneath her tight scrutiny, but was determined to have this conversation so they would stop badgering him. "Brooklyn kept telling me that a relationship was impossible. Then I remembered how she'd stormed over to Evan's house that night, and Evan coming back. Suddenly, everything made perfect sense. They still love each other."

"Did she tell you that?" Randall asked.

"Did she have to? She kept offering me everything but her heart. There's a reason for that, don't you think?"

Yasmine shrugged. "Yeah. Maybe she was just afraid of getting hurt again . . . just like you. Either way, with your leaving the way you did, we will never know the answer to that question, will we?"

Isaiah slid his hands into his pockets. "I believe I have my answer. I've been gone for nearly a month. If I was wrong, she would have called by now."

Twenty-eight

In early November, Evan surprised Brooklyn when he attended Sunday morning church service. Before she knew it, she heard their names whispered from the lips of people around them. It was Jaleel's first appearance in the choir since his accident, and she quickly assumed Evan came for support. But when he joined her and Toni in their pew, her suspicion changed.

The moment service ended, Sister Loretha swooshed up to them like a hawk after its prey. "I knew you two would get back together," she gushed. "I can't tell you how good it does my heart to see you guys as a family again."

Before Brooklyn corrected her, Evan cut in. "Thank you, Sister. Sometimes it takes a tragedy to get you to realize what you've lost."

Brooklyn elbowed him.

"Amen," Sister Loretha said with a grand show of approval.

But Brooklyn could tell she was just dying to know what had happened to Isaiah. When she'd brought him to church this summer, Loretha positively fawned over him.

However, Big Trouble Freddie quickly joined the group, and Brooklyn felt the beginnings of a headache.

"My brother, my brother." Freddie pounded Evan hard on the back. "It's good to see that you've finally come to your senses."

"Better late than never, I always say." Evan laughed and swung his arm around Brooklyn.

She elbowed him again and impaled him with a murderous glare before turning her emotionless smile toward Freddie and Sister Loretha. "Actually, we're just—"

"Here to support Jaleel." Evan squeezed her shoulder.

She caught his hint to roll with everyone's assumptions. Most likely it was because he didn't want to be embarrassed by the truth. But what about the embarrassment he'd caused her? She jabbed him again.

Evan lowered his arm.

Freddie rocked his enormous weight on the balls of his feet as he laughed. "You know, I was a little worried when I saw Brooklyn and that gray-eyed pretty boy in here this summer. You couldn't have slid a slip of paper between them, I tell ya. And this is the Lord's house, too." He chuckled.

Evan's smile disappeared.

Sister Loretha's mocha complexion turned a deep burgundy as her eyes darted uneasily around the small group. "Well, it's good seeing you both. I have a few things I need to discuss with the reverend before he leaves." She smiled awkwardly and avoided eye contact with Freddie.

Brooklyn's quick prayer for help was answered when Toni and Brian appeared at her side.

Freddie quickly excused himself, while Toni muttered "Pimp" from behind him.

"I'm starting to see why you can't stand that man," Evan said, glowering.

Toni huffed and crossed her arms. "It'll take a lot more than fancy clothes and a bottle of anointing oil for him to impress me."

Jaleel joined the group with the use of his cane. The long, jagged scar above his left ear was still visible. His extensive hours with the physical therapist had paid off, and he was beginning to move about like his former self.

Brooklyn leaned over and kissed him. "Honey, you looked great up there."

"You sure did." Evan moved closer and draped his arm around his son.

Jaleel thanked them though his face flushed with embarrassment. "Are you ready to go home, Mom?"

"Sure."

"Well, I was thinking we could all go out for lunch together," Evan said with a confident smile.

Brooklyn hesitated. "Not today. We have a lot to do this evening."

The rejection stole the radiance from Evan's

smile. "Then perhaps dinner—one day this week? Surely you guys could make time for that?"

She favored him with a smile. "We'll see."

Isaiah expelled a frustrated sigh into the phone as he talked to his mother. "Mom, I just think it would be better if you moved out here. I'm constantly worrying about you."

"Good heavens, why?"

"What if you have another stroke?"

"And my moving to Texas is going to prevent that?" she countered with humorous doubt.

"With you here, I can make sure that you're taking it easy."

"And how are you going to do that? You're constantly traveling. No, I'd rather stay here. Atlanta is my home. Besides, Rotech has an office here. Why don't you move here if you're so concerned?"

Isaiah placed his head into his hand and pinched the bridge of his nose. Returning to Atlanta was like returning to heartbreak. "Why can't you be reasonable about this?"

Georgia's soft laugh filtered through the phone line. "I could say the same thing about you."

Brooklyn moved through life happy to have her son back home, and miserable for having lost Isaiah. It was good that he'd left, she told herself. It had to end some time; now was just as good as later. She'd crammed his torn shirt into the bottom of her drawer along with all the sexy lingerie she'd bought for his eyes only. But not even those desperate acts could wipe him from her memory . . . or from her heart.

Every night he came to her in her dreams with twinkling gray eyes and a mischievous smile. She remembered vividly the clean taste and smell of his skin. Her body ached for his touch just as her mind obsessed over his leaving.

Her friends worried excessively over her, while her colleagues insisted that she had become quiet and distant. She gave everyone the same pat answer: "I'm fine."

Finally, one afternoon, Toni cornered her while she cooked dinner.

"You're not fine." Toni slammed her hand down on the counter. "Will you *please* stop saying that?"

Brooklyn ignored the outburst and continued to dump ingredients into her homemade vegetable stew.

Toni ranted on. "Look at you. The fact that you won't even *talk* about this is proof that something is wrong."

"There's nothing to talk about," Brooklyn said without looking up.

"So I'm supposed to believe that you're not the least bit upset about Isaiah leaving?"

She didn't answer.

"Well?"

Brooklyn slammed a metal spoon onto the counter, and then glared at Toni. "What I *need* is for you to let it go. It's over. And I'm tired of everyone trying to fix my life. That's how I got in this mess in the first place."

"Why don't you just call him?"

Brooklyn tossed her hands up in the air, astounded that Toni hadn't heard a word she'd said. "You know, if you spent half as much time worrying about your own problems as you do with mine, you just might have something that resembles a life."

Toni blinked. "O-o-okay. You're upset."

"No, Toni. I'm pissed. I should have known better than to listen to you or the other girls. What the hell do any of you know about relationships? None of you have been married before; none of you know what it feels like to invest your heart and soul into someone."

"Wait a minute. That's not fair—"

"Life isn't fair. Love isn't fair. Or maybe you're going to suggest another box of Band-Aids for my broken heart." Tears stung Brooklyn's eyes. "I didn't want to go through this again. I vowed never to go through this again." She clasped a hand across her trembling lips as tears spilled down her face.

"Brooklyn." Toni moved toward her.

She jumped back. "Just leave me alone." She rushed around her friend and dashed out of the kitchen.

Twenty-nine

Thanksgiving Day

Isaiah returned to Atlanta. It was, after all, tradition. So far, despite his best effort, Isaiah had been unable to convince his mother to move to Austin, and she protested against any talk of his moving to Atlanta on her account. So in the end, they'd developed a stalemate.

At the door, Georgia greeted him with an exuberant smile along with a houseful of guests.

Being back in Atlanta, Isaiah's thoughts of Brooklyn multiplied, and his urge to see her again consumed him. More than once, his mother caught him with his mind wandering.

"Sweetheart, are you okay?" she asked, finding him off in a corner.

He turned from the window and flashed her a reassuring smile. "I'm fine, Mom. Just thinking about work," he lied. "It doesn't help that I lost my cell phone at the airport."

She smiled. "You know, dinner won't start for

another hour or so. Why don't you go out for a drive or something? It'll clear your head."

He caught the hint and laughed. But when he opened his mouth to decline the suggestion, no words came out. He had to see Brooklyn, even if it was from a distance. "Maybe a drive is just what I need."

Brooklyn's sanity was in serious jeopardy. While her mother preached second chances, Toni lectured on the opposite. Through it all, no one asked what Brooklyn wanted or how she felt—and she was sick of it.

As the three women rushed to get dinner on the table, Brooklyn blocked out the women's incessant chatter. Why had she invited Evan for Thanksgiving dinner, especially when she'd invited her parents? Everyone had the wrong idea—including Evan.

Brian arrived and brought his tried-and-true potato salad, while Jaleel's girlfriend, Theresa, showed up with a sweet potato pie. That made six pies and counting.

"I swear I spend the whole year working off the damage I do between Thanksgiving and New Year's," Toni mumbled under her breath as she nibbled from the tray of hors d'ouvres.

Brooklyn smiled. "If I get through this night, it'll be a miracle." A hand landed on her shoulder, and she turned toward a smiling Jaleel.

"You need any help in here?" he asked.

"No. I think we have everything." She marveled over how handsome he looked. To her, he no longer held a youthful innocence in his features. He'd seemed to age years in a matter of months.

Toni picked up a few trays and took them out to the guests.

"Are you all right, Mom?"

Her smile weakened at the question. "What do you mean?"

He shrugged, but the gesture did nothing to alleviate the seriousness of his expression. "I don't know. Are you happy?"

Her smile flat-lined. "Yes, of course." She shrugged. "The family is all here, and you're doing great." She gestured at his tall stance. "Look at you. You're not using your cane today."

His gaze lowered as if she hadn't truly answered his question. "You don't have to do it for me, you know," he said, lifting his eyes again. "I heard you talking to Grandma earlier. If you do care for someone else, then don't go back to Dad for me."

Brooklyn held his intense gaze until she felt the sting of tears. "You're a good son."

He shrugged. "Yeah, well, I do what I can." He leaned over and kissed her before grabbing the bowl of three-bean salad and waltzing out to the table.

A few minutes later, Evan's parents showed up, and Jaleel stole their attention, to Brooklyn's great relief.

Needing a few minutes of reprieve before dinner, she sneaked outside. The cold, late-autumn air cleared her mind instantly as she drew in a breath and closed her eyes. Isaiah smiled back from her memory and said, "Nothing is impossible."

She opened her eyes just as a car approached and pulled up to claim the last spot in the driveway.

"Hello, Brooke."

"Hi, Evan," she said, walking out to greet him.

Stepping out of his car, he immediately enveloped her into his arms and placed a small kiss against her cheek. "I'm sorry I'm late. There was a small emergency at the hospital. Is everyone inside?"

"Yep."

"I guess that's why you're out here."

She laughed. "Yep." She quivered from the cold.

Evan removed his leather jacket and draped it around her shoulders.

"Thanks," she said, surprised by his gallantry.

"You used to like the holidays."

"Hmmph." She shook her head. "I used to like a lot of things. Time has a way of changing a person."

He studied her. "You're talking about us, aren't you?"

She nodded, and then made sure she met his gaze. "We can never go back, Evan. You have to know that."

His eyes turned toward the sky as pain pinched his features.

She went on. "We'll always have a common bond through Jaleel, but we don't have a future."

Evan nodded, and she could see the sheen of tears in his eyes.

"It's just as well," he said. "I don't deserve your forgiveness."

"Oh, I forgive you." She lifted her chin. "I had to in order to move on." She laughed at what she'd just said. "Someone told me that once, and he was right, but I want us to be friends. After all, we do have a son, and we're always going to be a part of his life."

He listened and then confessed, "I don't know how to be alone." He met her gaze again. "You were right about that."

She shook her head and reflected over the past two years. "You'll do fine."

He looked doubtful. "Can I ask you a question?"

"Sure."

"Are you still in love with him?"

She felt the threat of tears surface while she weighed telling him the truth. "Yes."

He sighed and draped an arm around her shoulders. "Then he's a lucky man."

Isaiah watched Brooklyn and Evan as they walked arm-in-arm back into the house before he started his car and drove away.

Nothing Is
Impossible . . .

Thirty

In early December, Brooklyn's schedule grew even more hectic. Her days were never long enough, and her nights remained haunted by a gray-eyed lover, which was why she dozed off in the waiting room of Gwinnett Hospital during Jaleel's physical therapy appointment.

Her exhaustion stemmed from constantly trying to be in three places at one time: work, home, and the hospital. With her annual trip to New York just two weeks away, she gave serious thought to whether she should even bother going this year.

She stirred at the light tap on her shoulder and reluctantly tried to wake up. She blocked a wide yawn with her hand as her eyes fluttered open to greet her son, but she was instead startled to see a smiling Georgia Washington. "Hi," Brooklyn said, suddenly alert.

"It looks like someone didn't get enough sleep," Georgia said, laughing.

Brooklyn's cheeks burned with embarrassment. "Something like that." She flashed her a smile in an attempt to mask the awkward tension. "So, how have you been?"

Georgia's smile brightened as she sat in the plastic chair next to Brooklyn. "Oh, I guess I can't complain. How about yourself?"

"Same, I guess," Brooklyn answered evasively. Georgia held her smile even as her eyes seemed to dissect Brooklyn's farcical expression.

"And how is your son doing?" Georgia finally asked, her voice maintaining its sincerity.

"Great." Brooklyn shifted in her chair. She couldn't shake the feeling of being in the witness stand and that at any moment she was going to trap herself in a lie. At the same time, it was killing her not to inquire about Isaiah.

"And you and your husband's reconciliation— how's that going?"

"What?" The question burst from Brooklyn with a note of amusement.

Georgia's smile faltered as her brows gathered to reflect her confusion. "You two aren't getting back together?"

"Heavens, no." Brooklyn shook her head and almost asked what had given Georgia such an idea, when the memory of Isaiah's letter floated back to her consciousness. "So what brings you here? Are you feeling all right?" she asked instead, in an attempt to shift the conversation from her.

Georgia waved her hand dismissively. "Oh, heavens, yes. I'm fine. Though I can't convince Isaiah otherwise." There. She'd said his name. Georgia watched Brooklyn with the intensity of a hawk.

Brooklyn's mistake came when she broke eye

contact. But the other choice would have been to allow Georgia to see the sudden gloss to her eyes.

Georgia's soft chuckle recaptured Brooklyn's attention.

"Pride is never your friend when it comes to love, honey. I'd have thought you and Isaiah would've learned that by now."

Brooklyn's heart squeezed while another wave of tears embarrassed her by sliding from her eyes. "You have an amazing knack for making complicated matters seem so simple."

"Or . . . you guys have an amazing ability to make something so simple complicated." She smiled. "Since you're not going to ask, I'll tell you this: He's miserable without you."

Brooklyn closed her eyes, overwhelmed by how much that little information affected her.

"Do you love him?" Georgia asked in a near whisper.

Brooklyn's eyes fluttered open. It was time for her to be honest—with Georgia and with herself. "More than anything."

"Great." Georgia draped an arm around Brooklyn's shoulders and squeezed with more strength than Brooklyn thought her capable. "Get out a pen—I think it's past time you had Isaiah's home number. I have a feeling he would be happy to hear from you."

Delta flight number 22 from Charles De Gaulle International Airport felt like the longest flight in history, thanks to the child with the healthy lungs in the back of the plane. Isaiah had popped his last two Excedrin more than an hour before and his temples still throbbed with the force of a jackhammer. He tried meditating, counting, and praying, but the child continued to wail. Finally, he turned his attention to the large clouds below the plane and tried to concentrate on how beautiful the sky appeared.

"Isaiah?"

Startled from his reverie, he jerked his head around and was surprised to see Cadence smiling back at him. God's sense of humor had just turned wicked.

"I knew it was you." Her eyes sparkled back at him before she gestured to the vacant seat next to him. "Mind if I join you?"

Isaiah opened his mouth, but she chose not to wait for an answer and dropped into the seat next to him.

"Let me guess. You're on your way home from another business trip."

He forced a plastic smile as the screaming kid showed his first sign of tiring. "You know me."

"Better than you ever gave me credit for." Her direct gaze held his, and then, as though an afterthought, she smiled. "How long have you been gone this time?"

He drew in a deep breath. "Since the day after Thanksgiving."

"Nearly three weeks?"

"Yep," he responded with a plastic smile.

"I guess that sort of tells me why I couldn't reach you two weeks ago. I threw your uncle a surprise birthday party. I think he would have liked it if you had come."

"I've lost my cell phone. I haven't had a chance to replace it yet." Even if he had it, he doubted he would have attended the party.

"You know, you're all your uncle has left of his younger brother. You could try to be a little kinder toward him."

Isaiah's temples throbbed harder as Cadence managed to make him feel guilty.

"So," she went on as if she hadn't noticed his silence, "I heard through the grapevine you were suffering from a broken heart."

Isaiah didn't have time to hide his shock. "Who told you that?"

"Randall."

He closed his eyes and cursed his friend's indiscretion. "Randall has a big mouth."

"No news flash there," she agreed, her smile broadening.

Isaiah's eyes narrowed. "Is that the real reason you came over here—to gloat?"

Cadence opened her mouth, no doubt to deny such a thing, but then appeared to have thought better of it. "Maybe you know me pretty well, too."

He nodded and could feel his smile turn genuine.

"So who is the lucky woman?"

"You expect me to tell you?"

"I don't see why not. We have at least four more

hours on this flight, and I don't have anything better to do." She smiled again.

He shook his head and looked straight ahead. The funny thing was, Isaiah began to believe her friendly attitude toward him was sincere. "Why would you want to hear about it—other than to gloat? I was under the distinct impression that you hated me." From the corner of his eyes, he caught her light shrug and smile.

"I wouldn't say that I hate you . . . exactly."

He faced her again. "Oh?" He laughed as he crossed his arms. "What exactly would you say?"

"I would say that I've been angry with you for a long time—too long, in fact."

Isaiah lowered his gaze, unsure of what he should say. He drew in a deep breath. "Her name is Brooklyn Douglas," he finally said with his lips curling into a smile again.

To Cadence's credit, she continued to look at him. "And you're in love with her?"

He squirmed in his seat. The awkwardness of having this conversation with her wasn't easy to ignore. "Yeah."

If the conversation bothered Cadence, she did a good job of hiding it. "Does she know how you feel, or is it some great secret?"

He cut a narrowed look in her direction. "What is that supposed to mean?"

She shrugged. "Nothing. Just that when we were together, you kept your emotions close to your vest."

He let go of the edginess he held in his voice. "I'm sorry about that."

She reached over and touched his hand. "Don't be. It was a long time ago. And whether you choose to believe it or not, I'm quite happy with the man I married."

Isaiah studied her. "You really love him?"

"More than life itself," she answered without hesitation.

He covered her hand with his. "In that case, I'm happy for you."

"Great. So what's the problem?"

"Who said there was a problem?"

She stared at him and waited.

Isaiah shrugged as he released an exaggerated sigh. "I don't know what I was thinking. It would've never worked out. I'm married to my job, remember?"

"Painfully."

He frowned. "I got caught up in a fantasy and playing a game I had no business playing."

"Randall said you were simply waiting for her to call."

He rolled his eyes and made a mental note to kill his good friend. "Well, he was wrong. After having so much time to reflect, my walking away was the best thing for both of us. At this point, I don't think a call would do it. It's over."

Thirty-one

New York

"I say the hell with him," Maria said, rolling her eyes. "It's his loss if he doesn't come tonight."

Brooklyn shared a lopsided grin but found no comfort in her friend's over-the-top attempt to cheer her up. In fact, she wished everyone would just change the subject. She was nervous enough without their help.

For the past few weeks she'd called Isaiah's home and left him messages. He had yet to return any of them. Then she had gotten this crazy idea that they should meet in New York on the anniversary of their first meeting—in the same bar, at the same time.

If he came, it meant he was willing to give their love another try. If he didn't—well, she didn't want to think about him not showing up.

"I hate to say it." Toni regained Brooklyn's attention. "But I agree with Maria. A woman can only do so much begging."

Brooklyn jumped on the defensive. "I'm not begging."

Her girlfriends fell silent.

"Whatever." Annoyed, Brooklyn crossed her arms. Maybe she'd gone a little overboard with the number of messages she'd left on Isaiah's answering machine. But what do you do when you're trying to stop the best thing that ever happened to you from walking out of your life forever?

"He'll show up," she said, careful to avoid their gazes. "I just know he will."

December had very little effect on Texas's weather. Had it not been for the holiday decorations in busy Bergstrom Airport, the day would have seemed like any other.

The flight in from France taxed Isaiah's mind as well as his body, though it was good to be back in Austin. Life had been odd since he'd lost his cell phone—wonderful, but odd.

It was also weird watching Cadence's excitement when she spotted his uncle Mike waiting for her. It was stranger still to walk over to him and have their first real civil conversation in more than two years.

After locating his luggage in baggage claim, Isaiah climbed into the first available taxi and took a nap during the drive to his house.

Once home, it took his remaining strength to carry his bags up the arching staircase to his bedroom. If he could just catch a few hours of sleep, he'd be okay, he told himself. However, reason said he needed a minimum of ten hours.

He stripped out of his clothes and seconds later stood beneath a pounding stream of hot water. He had to stop punishing himself with this crazy work schedule, but not until he could forget about Brooklyn.

Stepping out of the shower, Isaiah dried off and slid into his favorite robe. The phone rang, but he paid it no attention. Whoever it was could leave a message.

"Now, sleep," he said as he clicked off the bathroom light and re-entered his bedroom, but the sound of Brooklyn's voice stopped him in his tracks.

"I guess you're still avoiding me." Her voice held a dreary sigh. "Look, I hope you come or, who knows, maybe you're on your way up here." She paused, and then added wearily, "If you don't show up tonight, I'll know it's over." Another pause. "I love you, Isaiah. Please come." The call disconnected.

Isaiah remained rooted in place. *She loves me?* Surely, he hadn't heard her right. Slowly her message seeped into his brain and he became more confused. "Show up where?" he muttered and he walked over to the answering machine and pushed the play button.

The robotic voice reported: "You have sixty-two messages."

* * *

Walking through the doors of the Atrium, Brooklyn experienced a jolt of déjà vu. This time, she didn't feel out of place. She felt more like a woman on a mission, and she experienced a pleasant surprise when she recognized the smiling bartender.

He inclined his head, but recognition eluded his eyes.

She strolled up to the bar, needing very much to have a drink.

"Good evening, miss. What can I get you?"

"An apple margarita."

"Excellent choice."

"I know. You make a mean one."

A light flickered in his eyes. "Have you been here before?"

Suddenly she was embarrassed at just how much the man could or would remember. "It's been a while."

He nodded. "One apple margarita coming up."

She sighed in relief and nervously glanced around the dark and crowded lounge. Her heart accelerated whenever her eyes skimmed over a similar physique and then plummeted when it turned out not to be Isaiah.

"He's not coming," the devil on her shoulder whispered. And why should he? Hadn't she done everything she could to keep him at arm's length?

The bartender returned with a wide smile. "So. Why the long face?" He set her drink down.

She shrugged. "I'm sort of waiting for someone."

He nodded with a look of instant understanding. "And you're worried whether he'll show up?"

Brooklyn managed a crooked smile. "Boy, I bet you've seen and heard it all working here."

"Pretty much. I know enough to know a man would have to be crazy to stand up a beautiful woman like you."

She blushed. "It's a little more complicated than that."

"All love stories are."

"Is it that obvious?"

"Just to an experienced eye." He winked.

Her smile warmed, but she said nothing as her mood continued to free-fall.

He fixed two gin and tonics, and a looming cocktail waitress quickly snatched them up. "Want to talk about it?" he asked Brooklyn.

"So you're a bartender-slash-therapist?"

"Most of us are."

"Then I guess you qualify." A sad laugh escaped her as she lowered her gaze and reached for her glass. "Problem is I don't know where to begin."

"The beginning—there is always a beginning."

So, that was what she did; and once she started, she couldn't stop.

And like any good therapist, Sam the bartender listened while simultaneously mixing drinks.

At the end, he stopped and placed his hands flat on the bar's counter. "Then tonight is your moment of truth."

She glanced at her watch only to be devastated by the time. "It was." Her sigh accompanied a fresh surge of tears. "I should have known better." She stood from her chair; ready to call it a night.

"I said from the beginning that the whole thing was impossible."

She turned for a final glance around the lounge and drew in a sharp gasp at Isaiah's sudden appearance at her side.

"Haven't you learned by now that nothing is impossible?"

Brooklyn's breath thinned as her hand settled across her heart. "You came."

His lips curved and flashed her a beautiful smile. "Of course."

She couldn't stop staring, too afraid to blink, breathe, or think. "I love you," she blurted out.

He stepped forward with a slow nod and smile. "Yeah. I got your messages." He leaned down and brushed his lips lightly over hers. "I love you, too."

The bartender snickered. "I just love happy endings."

Isaiah and Brooklyn laughed.

"So is this when I offer to buy the lady a drink?" he asked, amusement conquering his features.

Brooklyn shrugged and eased closer. "Yes, or we could just skip the small talk and continue this happy reunion up in your suite," she suggested boldly.

Isaiah blinked away his surprise. "My suite?" Suspicion narrowed his gaze as disappointment webbed his heart.

Brooklyn rolled her eyes heavenward while her posture deflated. "I'm doing it again, aren't I?"

He nodded as he took her hand. "We need to talk."

"I know." A weak smile fluttered at the corners of her lips before she returned to her stool.

Isaiah eased onto the seat next to her. For a few seconds, he just stared at her delicate features and feared her response to what he had to say.

Brooklyn slyly broke eye contact. "I think I should go first."

Isaiah pretended he didn't feel the squeeze to his heart. "All right."

She took a deep breath and plunged ahead. "I didn't invite you here for a repeat performance." She found his gaze again, but words stalled in her throat as she collected herself to continue. "I wanted you to come, because for the past few months I've been forced to realize just how much you truly mean to me. And the truth is, you're my world. I want you to be a part of my life."

Relief poured into Isaiah's body. Her declaration caused his heart to take flight. "It seems like I've waited forever to hear you say that." His laugh cracked with emotion.

Her gaze softened. "I'm relieved to finally get the chance to tell you in person. Of course, I think I've developed a close and personal relationship with your answering machine."

"Sounds like I should be jealous."

"Don't be. I'm just glad your mother talked some sense into me."

Surprise colored Isaiah's features. "My mother?"

"Yeah." Her smile widened. "She's a very wise woman."

"Let me guess. The pride speech?"

"You've heard it?"

"Heard it. It's one of my favorites."

As their laughter faded, Brooklyn squeezed his hand affectionately. "I'm so glad you came."

"I've missed you." His hand lifted to caress the curve of her cheek.

She kissed his hand. "I've been so miserable without you that even my son has granted us his blessing. In fact, he can't wait to meet you."

"I can't wait to meet him, too." He lifted her hand, kissed it, and then took a deep breath. "With that said, there's something I want to ask you."

The seriousness in his voice matched the intensity of his gaze, and Brooklyn's heart pounded in double time.

He slid his hand into his pocket and withdrew a burgundy box. "I meant to ask you this a few months ago."

Brooklyn's eyes widened at the sight of what could only be a ring box and once again felt her eyes sting with tears. "Oh, my God."

He leaned in for another kiss, and then opened the box.

She gasped at the sparkling diamond ring.

"The night of Jaleel's accident, I was trying my damnedest to propose and could never get the words out. So tonight, before we go any further, I have to ask: will you marry me?"

Words deserted Brooklyn.

"I want to be clear about this," Isaiah continued. "I don't want just your body. I want you. Forever."

"But we live in different states," she finally protested weakly.

"I'll move."

"What about your job?"

"I can transfer or look for a new one." He smiled when she ran out of questions and tears trickled down her face. He wiped them away with his thumbs. "I will do whatever it takes to be with you."

Brooklyn drew in a deep breath and met his twinkling gray eyes. "So will I."

"Is that a yes?"

"Absolutely."

Isaiah shouted with joy as he swept her off the stool and into his arms. He'd done it. He had finally won Brooklyn Douglas's heart.

"Let's get out of here and celebrate." Giddy, Brooklyn turned to take care of her tab.

The bartender held up his hand and winked. "It's on the house. Enjoy your evening."

Brooklyn had every intention of doing just that.

The newly engaged couple walked out of the Atrium with their arms nestled around each other. There were no words needed for their destination.

Everything about Isaiah was just as Brooklyn remembered: the build, the smell, and the feel of him.

Stepping into the elevator, she slinked into a corner of the glass compartment and motioned for him to follow with a sexy come-hither look. Isaiah obeyed, fully aware that they could be seen in the glass compartment.

"Wait. Hold the elevator," a woman's voice boomed toward them.

With lightning speed, Isaiah jabbed the close-door button.

Brooklyn burst out laughing as the door closed in front of a stunned woman. "Ooh, you're soo bad."

He pressed for the twenty-third floor and returned to cuddle in their corner. "I'm just determined for nothing to ruin our night."

"Nothing could ruin this night."

In practice for their honeymoon, Isaiah carried Brooklyn across the threshold of his suite. And this time he took his time undressing her.

Brooklyn's body was on fire, consumed by passion and love. And it felt wonderful—it felt right.

Minutes passed before she noticed the red and white rose petals across the floor. Soft music played from the radio on the nightstand alongside a bottle of champagne that chilled in a silver bucket of ice.

"You came prepared."

"I did what I could on such short notice."

She frowned. "Short notice?"

"I've been away on business for the past three weeks. I got your messages today."

"Ah, that explains a lot." She kissed him.

He nuzzled her neck, finding that old switch that melted her insides and branded her.

Together they fell back onto the bed, and Isaiah easily claimed the top position.

At the feel of his hardened desire pressed against her inner thigh, she reined in her raging emotions to ask the all-important question. "You do have a condom, right?"

Isaiah slumped against her as he lowered his head.

Brooklyn slapped a hand across her face as laughter burst from her lungs.

Slowly a mischievous smile dominated Isaiah's features as he reached across the bed and opened the nightstand drawer to reveal that it was crammed tight with boxes of condoms.

"I think we have just enough," he said.

Brooklyn's laughter deepened as she slid her arms around his neck. "Yeah. Just enough."

Epilogue

Six months later

Rotech's Golden Circle Award ceremony was being held in the lavish Embassy Suites in Autin, Texas. The guests were beautiful, distinguished, and successful. Many complimented and enjoyed the royal treatment Rotech provided while they congratulated and hobnobbed with the new Man of the year, Yasmine Hewitt.

Isaiah and Brooklyn Washington approached their glowing friend with outstretched arms.

"I can't believe this night," Yasmine gushed as she stepped back. "I don't see why you used to hate it so much."

Isaiah shrugged. "Hey, if you like it, I love it." He gave her an affectionate squeeze. "You deserve this, Yas."

"Damn right, I do." She laughed.

Randall dipped into the group and gave Yasmine a hug as well. "I guess this means I have a shot next year."

"I don't know. Now that I've had a taste of stardom, I don't know if I want to give it up."

"Congratulations." Brooklyn leaned in and kissed Yasmine's cheek. "I'm so happy for you."

Yasmine jiggled her brows at Isaiah. "You better watch this one. I might steal her away from you."

They laughed just as a feminine voice floated from behind them.

"I heard that."

The small group turned and spotted Yasmine's off-again, on-again girlfriend, Mary.

"I was just teasing," Yasmine apologized.

Mary joined the group and received her fair share of hugs before pulling back to assess Brooklyn. "There is something different about you."

Brooklyn tried to fight back the telling smile from dominating her face.

"What?" Yasmine's gaze swung between Isaiah and Brooklyn. "Something is up. Spill it."

Isaiah draped an arm around Brooklyn's shoulders. "Well, we didn't want to take anything away from your night."

"But?" Yasmine's eyes sparkled as though she already suspected the news.

"We're pregnant," Isaiah and Brooklyn announced, and in the next second were crushed in their friends' exuberant hugs. A minute later, Cadence and Uncle Mike joined them and gave their well-wishes.

Later that night, Brooklyn lay awake in Isaiah's arms and watched the subtle rise and fall of his chest. She reveled in the peace he helped create in her life.

Despite being a part of a unit, Isaiah allowed her to maintain her independence as a career woman. She had opened her own realty office back in the spring and had no doubts that she would continue even after delivering her next bundle of joy.

She stood from the bed and moved over to the window. The streets weren't as busy as Times Square or Peachtree Street, but there was something to be said for the city's serenity. She no longer minded the sun coming up because she now enjoyed every aspect of her life.

She couldn't believe that, while Jaleel was preparing to go to college, she was getting ready for a new baby at forty. But regardless, she was happy.

The sound of footsteps approaching from behind didn't startle her, neither did the pair of arms enfolding her, but the gentle kiss against her neck won a sly smile.

"What are you thinking about?" Isaiah asked, nuzzling her neck again.

She leaned back to press against his hard, naked body. "How can a girl think with you doing that?"

"Doing what?" He rained a trail of kisses along her shoulder.

She turned toward him and slid her arms around his neck. "You've made me so happy."

"The pleasure is mine every minute of the day."

Brooklyn leaned up on her toes and slowly kissed the lids of his eyes, the tip of his nose, and then finally extracted a long mind-shattering kiss. "Are you up for another round?"

"Do you even have to ask?" He laughed, swooped her up in his arms, and carried her back to bed.